High Pr...
'TOP of the HEAP'!

"An ingenious story."
— *Kirkus Reviews*

"One of the best in the series… An illegal casino, bogus mines, former strippers and dead bodies abound… You can only love a book where everyone gets exactly what they deserve in triplicate."
— *Karen Ellington, The Mystery Read*

"A fine elaborate business of stock manipulation and (to fit in with the current worries of us all) income tax deception."
— *Anthony Boucher, The New York Times*

"It's a neatly knotted puzzle and Donald unties it very neatly, too."
— *New York Herald Tribune Book Review*

"A fast-paced, action-packed story."
— *Springfield Republican*

Rave Reviews for
Erle Stanley GARDNER!

The blonde nervously took a cigarette case from a black bag and tapped the cigarette on the side of the polished silver. I snapped a match into flame, and she leaned forward for the light. I could see the long curling eyelashes, the mischievous glint of saucy hazel eyes, as she looked me over.

"Thank you," she said.

Abruptly the floor manager glided up to the table. His smile was reassuring. "I have been asked," he said, "to invite you to step into the office, Miss Marvin, and the boss would like to see Mr. Lam, too."

The floor manager escorted us deferentially to a big door marked Private. He didn't come in. The door clicked shut behind us. I turned to look. There was no knob on the door.

Channing shook hands with both of us. "How are you, Lam?" he said.

"Fine," I told him.

I didn't see Channing give the signal, but abruptly the door from the outer office opened and a man in a tuxedo stood quietly on the threshold.

"Mr. Lam," Channing said, "had a card when he entered the place. He doesn't wish to produce that card. I'd like very much to look at it."

The newcomer reached forward and grabbed my wrist. I tried to jerk the arm free. I might as well have tried to pull against a steel cable.

Swift, efficient fingers did things to the wrist. The other hand hit against my elbow. My arm doubled around, flew up against my back, the wrist doubled into a grip that pulled the tendons until it was all I could do to keep from screaming.

"The card," Channing said...

TOP of
the HEAP

by Erle Stanley Gardner

WRITING UNDER THE NAME 'A. A. FAIR'

A HARD CASE CRIME NOVEL

A HARD CASE CRIME BOOK

(HCC-003)

October 2004

Published by

Dorchester Publishing Co., Inc.
200 Madison Avenue
New York, NY 10016

in collaboration with Winterfall LLC

ISBN 0-8439-5352-7

The name "Hard Case Crime" and the Hard Case Crime logo
are trademarks of Winterfall LLC. Hard Case Crime Books are
selected and edited by Charles Ardai.

Printed in the United States of America

Visit us on the web at www.HardCaseCrime.com

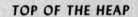

TOP OF THE HEAP

Chapter One

I was in the outer office, standing by the files, doing some research on a blackmailer, when he came in, all six feet of him.

He wore a plaid coat, carefully tailored, pleated slacks, and two-tone sport shoes. He was built like a secondhand soda straw, and I heard him say he wanted to see the senior partner. He said it with the air of a man who always demands the best, and then settles for what he can get.

The receptionist glanced at me hopefully, but I was deadpan. Bertha Cool was the "senior" partner.

"The *senior* partner?" she asked, still keeping an eye on me.

"That's right. I believe it is B. Cool," he announced, glancing toward the names painted on the frosted glass of the doorway to the reception room.

She nodded and plugged in to B. Cool's phone. "The name?" she asked.

He drew himself up importantly, whipped an alligator-skin card case from his pocket, took out a card, and presented it to her with a flourish.

She puzzled over it for a moment as though having difficulty getting it interpreted. "Mr. Billings?"

"Mr. John Carver Billings the—"

Bertha Cool answered the phone just then, and the girl said, "A Mr. Billings. A Mr. John Carver Billings to see you."

"The Second," he interposed, tapping the card. "Can't you read? The Second!"

"Oh, yes," she said, "the Second."

That evidently threw Bertha Cool for a loss. Apparently she wanted an explanation.

"The Second," the girl repeated into the phone. "It's on his card that way, and that's the way he says it. His name is

John Carver Billings, and then there are two straight lines after the Billings."

The man frowned impatiently. "Send my card in," he ordered.

The receptionist automatically ran her thumbnail over the engraving on the card and said, "Yes, Mrs. Cool," into the telephone.

Then she hung up and said to Billings, "Mrs. Cool will see you now. You may go right in."

"*Mrs.* Cool?" the man said.

"Yes."

"That's B. Cool?"

"Yes. B. for Bertha."

He hesitated perceptibly, then straightened his plaid sport coat and walked in.

The receptionist waited until the door had closed, then looked up at me and said, "He wants a man."

"No," I told her, "he wants the *senior* partner."

"When he asks for you what shall I tell him?"

I said, "You underestimate Bertha. She'll find out how much dough he has, and if it's a sizable chunk she'll ask me in for a conference. If it isn't a big wad and John Carver Billings the Second intimates he thinks a woman isn't as good a detective as a man, you'll see Mr. John Carver Billings the Second thrown out of here on his ear."

She looked very demure. "You're so careful with your anatomical distinctions, Mr. Lam," she said without smiling.

I went back to my office.

In about ten minutes the phone rang.

Elsie Brand, my secretary, answered, then glanced up and said, "Mrs. Cool wants to know if you can come into her office for a conference."

"Sure," I said, and gave the receptionist a wink as I walked past and opened the door of Bertha's private office.

One look at the expression on Bertha's face and I knew everything was fine. Bertha's little, greedy eyes were glittering. Her lips were all smiles. "Donald," she said, "this is John Carver Billings."

"The Second," he amended.

"The Second," she echoed. "And this is Mr. Donald Lam, my partner."

We shook hands.

I knew from experience that it took cold, hard cash to get Bertha to assume that ingratiating manner and that cooing, kittenish voice.

"Mr. Billings," she said, "has a problem. He feels that perhaps a man should work on that problem, that it might—"

"Be more conducive of results," John Carver Billings the Second finished.

"Exactly," Bertha agreed with a cash-inspired alacrity of good humor.

"What's the problem?" I asked.

Bertha's chair squeaked as she moved her hundred and sixty-five pounds around so as to pick up the newspaper clipping on the far corner of her desk. She handed it to me without a word.

I read:

KNIGHT DAY'S COLUMN—DAY AND NIGHT

BLOND BEAUTY DISAPPEARS. FRIENDS FEAR FOUL PLAY. POLICE SKEPTICAL.

Maurine Auburn, the blond beauty who was with "Gabby" Garvanza at the time he was shot, has mysteriously disappeared. "Friends" have asked police to make an investigation.

The police, however, who feel that the young woman was considerably less than co-operative during their investigation into the shooting of the mobster, are inclined to feel that Miss Auburn, who kept her own counsel so successfully a few nights ago, is about business of her own. So far as police are concerned, her failure to pick up milk bottles from the doorstep of her swank little bungalow in Laurel Canyon is a matter of official indifference. In fact, officers pointed out quite plainly that Miss Auburn resented having police "stick their noses" into her private life a few days ago, and the police intend to respect her desire for privacy whenever possible.

The story as given to police by "friends" is that three days ago Maurine Auburn, who was the life of the party at a well-known nitery, became peeved at her escort and walked out.

Nor did she walk out alone.

Her departure was prefaced by a few dances with a new acquaintance whom she had met for the first time at the night club. The fact that she left the place with this newfound friend, rather than with members of her own party, is a circumstance which police consider to be without especial significance. Friends of the young woman, however, regard it as a matter of the greatest importance. Detectives are frank to state they do not consider this occurrence unique in the life of the mysterious young woman who was so singularly unobservant when Gabby Garvanza was on the receiving end of two leaden slugs.

When milk bottles began to pile up on Miss Auburn's doorstep, the peeved and jilted escort, whose name is being withheld by the police, felt that something should be done. He went to the police—perhaps for the first time in his life. Prior to that time, as one of the officers expressed it, the police had gone to him.

In the meantime, Garvanza, who has so far recov-

ered that he has been definitely pronounced out of danger, continues to occupy a private room at a local hospital and, despite his convalescence, continues to employ three special nurses.

After coming out of an anesthetic at the hospital following the operation which resulted in removing two bullets from his body, Gabby Garvanza listened patiently to police inquiries, then, by way of helpful cooperation, said, "I reckon somebody who had it in for me must have taken a coupla shots at me."

Police consider this a masterly understatement of fact and point out that as an aid to investigative work it is somewhat less than a valuable contribution. There was a distinct feeling at headquarters that both Gabby Garvanza and Miss Auburn could have been much more helpful.

I dropped the clipping back on Bertha's desk and looked at John Carver Billings the Second.

"Honestly," he said, "I never knew who she was."

"You're the pickup?" I asked.

He nodded.

"And Maurine left the nitery with you?"

"It really wasn't a night club. This was late in the afternoon, a cocktail rendezvous, food and dancing."

I said to Bertha, "We *might* not want to handle this one."

Bertha's greedy eyes flashed at me. Her jeweled hand surreptitiously strayed toward the cash drawer. "Mr. Billings has paid us a retainer," she said.

"And I offer a five-hundred-dollar bonus," Billings went on.

"I was coming to that," Bertha interposed.

"A bonus for what?" I asked.

"If you can find the girls I was with afterward."

"After what?"

"After the Auburn girl left me."

"That same night?"

"Of course."

"You seem to have covered a lot of territory," I said.

"It was this way," Bertha explained. "Mr. Billings was to have been joined for cocktails by a young woman. This young woman stood him up. He had been attracted to Maurine Auburn, and, when he caught her eye, asked her to dance. One of the men who was with her told Billings to go roll his hoop. Miss Auburn told the guy *he* didn't own her, and he said he knew that; he was watching the premises for the man who did.

"It looked like the party might get rough so Billings, here, went back to his own table.

"A few minutes later Maurine Auburn came over to his table and said, 'Well, you asked for a dance, didn't you?'

"So they danced, and, as our client says, they clicked. He was nervous because her escorts looked like tough mugs. He suggested she shake them and have dinner with him. She told him about another place she liked. They went there. As far as Billings knows she's still powdering her nose."

"What did you do?" I asked Billings.

"I stuck around, feeling like a sap. Then I noticed two girls by themselves. I made a play for one of them and got the eye. We danced for a while. By that time I realized, of course, Maurine had stood me up. I wanted one of these girls to ditch the other one so we could go places. No dice. They were together and they were going to stay together. I moved over to their table, bought them a couple of drinks, danced with them, had dinner, paid the check, and took them to an auto court."

"Then what?"

"I stayed all night."

"Where?"

"In this motor court."

"With *both* of them?"

"They were in bedrooms. I was on a couch in the front room."

"Platonic?"

"We'd all had quite a bit to drink."

"Then what?"

"About ten-thirty in the morning we had tomato juice. The girls cooked up a breakfast. They weren't feeling too good and I was feeling like hell. I got away from there, went to my own motel, took a shower, and went down to a barbershop, got shaved and massaged and— Well, from there on I can account for my time."

"Every minute of it?"

"Every minute of it."

"Where was the motor court?"

"Out on Sepulveda."

Bertha said, "You see, Donald, these were a couple of San Francisco babes on an auto tour. Mr. Billings thinks they knew each other pretty well, that they may have been relatives, or may have been working together in an office somewhere. Apparently they'd planned an auto tour of the country on their vacation. They wanted to see a Hollywood night spot and see if they could get a glimpse of a movie star. When Mr. Billings offered to dance with them they were willing to play along but they were playing the cards close to their chest and wouldn't let the party split up.

"Mr. Billings offered to drive them in his car but they said they were going to drive their own car. He— Well, he didn't want to say good night too soon."

Billings looked at me and shrugged his shoulders. "One of these babes had gone for me, and I'd gone for her," he said. "I thought I might get rid of the chaperon if I tagged along. I didn't. I'd had a little more to drink than I thought. When we got out to the motor court I proposed a nightcap and— Well, either they loaded it on me or I'd already had too much. The next thing I knew I was all alone and then it was daylight and I had a beautiful hangover."

"How were the girls the next morning?"

"Sweet and cordial."

"Affectionate?"

"Don't be silly. They weren't in the mood any more than I was. We'd all of us been seeing the town."

"And what do you want?"

"I want to find those two girls."

"Why?"

"Because," Bertha said, "he's uneasy now that it seems Maurine Auburn has disappeared."

"Why beat about the bush?" Billings said. "She's Gabby's moll. She knows who pumped the lead into him. She didn't tell the police but she knows. Suppose someone should think that she told me?"

"Any particular reason why she should tell you?" I asked.

"Or," he said hastily, "suppose something's happened to her? Suppose the milk bottles keep on piling up on her porch?"

"Did Maurine Auburn give you her name?"

"No. She just told me I could call her 'Morrie.' It was when I saw her picture in the paper that I knew what I'd been up against.

"The guys with her must have been mobsters. Think of me barging up and asking for a dance!"

"Do that sort of thing often?" I asked.

"Certainly not. I'd been drinking, and I'd been stood up."

"And then you went out and picked up these two babes?"

"That's right, only they made it remarkably easy for me.

They were on the prowl themselves—just a couple of janes on a vacation looking for a little adventure."

"What names did they give you?" I asked.

"Just their first names, Sylvia and Millie."

"Who was the one that you fell for?"

"Sylvia, the little brunette."

"What did the other one look like?"

"A redhead who had a possessive complex as far as Sylvia was concerned. She knew all the answers and didn't want me asking questions. She built a barbed wire fence around Sylvia and kept her inside of it. She may have loaded my drink with something besides liquor. I don't know. Anyway, she produced the bottle for a nightcap and I went out like a light."

"They consented to let you take them home?"

"Yes. As a matter of fact, they hadn't checked in anywhere yet. They wanted a motor court."

"You went in their car?"

"That's right."

"Did they register when you got to this motor court?"

"No. They asked me to register. That was the nicest way of asking me to pay the bill. In a motor court you pay in advance."

"Were you driving their car?"

"No. Sylvia was driving the car. I was sitting in the front seat next to Millie."

"Millie was in the middle?"

"Yes."

"And you told Sylvia where to drive?"

"Yes. She wanted to know where to get a good motor court. I told her I'd try and get one for her."

"And you picked this court out on Sepulveda?"

"We passed up a couple that had a sign 'No Vacancy' but this one had a vacancy sign."

"You went in there?"

"Yes, we drove in."

"Who went to the office?"

"I did."

"And you registered?"

"Yes."

"How did you register?"

"I can't remember the name I thought of."

"Why didn't you use your own name?"

He looked at me scornfully and said, "You're a hell of a detective. Would you have used your name under the circumstances?"

"When it came to putting down the make and license number of the automobile what did you do?"

"There," he said with a burst of feeling, "is where I made the mistake. Instead of going out and getting the license number of their automobile I just made up one out of my head."

"And the person who was running the motor court didn't go out to check it?"

"Of course not. If you look reasonably respectable they never go out to check the license number. Sometimes they just check the make of the automobile and that's all."

"What make of car was it?"

"A Ford."

"And you registered it as a Ford?"

"Yes. Why all the third degree? If you don't want the case give me back my retainer and I'll be on my way."

Bertha Cool's eyes glittered. "Don't be silly. My partner is simply trying to get the facts of the case so we can help you."

"It sounds to me as though he's cross-examining me."

"He doesn't mean anything by it," Bertha said. "Donald will locate these girls for you. He's good."

"He'd better be," Billings said sullenly.

"Is there anything else," I asked, "that you can tell us that will help?"

"Not a thing."

"The address of the motor court?"

"I gave it to Mrs. Cool."

"What was the number of your cabin at the court?"

"I can't remember the number, but it was the one on the right at the far corner. I think it was Number Five."

I said, "Okay. We'll see what we can do."

Billings said, "Remember that if you find these women there's to be a five-hundred-dollar bonus."

I said, "That bonus business doesn't conform to the rules of ethics that are laid down for the operation of a private detective agency."

"Why not?" Billings asked.

"It makes it too much like operating on a contingency fee. They don't like it."

"Who doesn't like it?"

"The people who issue the licenses."

"All right," he said to Bertha, "you find the girls and I'll donate five hundred dollars to your favorite charity."

"Are you nuts?" Bertha asked.

"What do you mean?"

"My favorite charity," Bertha told him, "is *me.*"

"Your partner says contingency fees are out."

Bertha snorted.

"Well, no one's going to tell anyone about it," Billings said, "unless *you* get loquacious."

"It's okay by me," Bertha said.

I said, "I'd prefer to have it on a basis that—"

"You haven't found the girls yet," Billings interrupted. "Now get this straight. I want an alibi for that night. The only way I can get it is to find these girls. I want affidavits. I've made my proposition. I've given you all of the information that I have. I'm not accustomed to having my word questioned."

He glared at me, arose stiffly, and walked out.

Bertha looked at me angrily. "You damn near upset the applecart."

"Provided there is any applecart."

She tapped the cash drawer. "There's three hundred dollars in there. That makes it an applecart."

I said, "Then we'd better start looking for the rotten apples."

"There aren't any."

I said, "His story stinks."

"What do you mean?"

I said, "Two girls drive down from San Francisco, they want to look over Hollywood, and see if they can find a movie star dining out somewhere."

"So what? That's exactly what two women *would* do under the circumstances."

I said, "They'd driven down from San Francisco. The first thing they'd do would be to take a bath, unpack their suitcases, hook up a portable iron, run it over their clothes, freshen up with make-up, and *then* go looking for movie stars. The idea that they'd have driven all the way down from San Francisco and—"

"You don't know that they made it all in one day."

"All right, suppose they made it in two days. The idea that they'd have driven from San Luis Obispo or Bakersfield, or any other place, parked their car, and gone directly to a night club without stopping to make themselves as attractive as possible, stinks."

Bertha blinked her eyes over that one. "Perhaps they did all that but lied to Billings because they didn't want him to know where they were staying."

I said, "Their suitcases must have been in the car,

according to Billings's statement."

Bertha sat there in her squeaking swivel chair, her fingers drumming nervously on the top of the desk, making the light scintillate from the diamonds with which she had loaded her fingers. "For the love of Pete," she said, "get out and get on the job. What the hell do you think this partnership is, anyway? A debating society or a detective agency?"

"I was simply pointing out the obvious."

"Well, don't point it out to me," Bertha yelled. "Go find those two women. The five-hundred-bucks bonus is the obvious in this case as far as I'm concerned!"

"Did you," I asked, "get a description?"

She tore a sheet of paper from a pad on her desk and literally threw it at me. "There are all the facts," she said. "My God, why did I ever get a partner like you? Some son of a bitch with money comes in and you start antagonizing him. And a five-hundred-dollar bonus, too."

I said, "I don't suppose it ever occurred to you to ask him who John Carver Billings the First might have been?"

Bertha screamed, "What the hell do I care who he is, just so John Carver Billings the Second has money? Three hundred dollars in cold, hard cash. No check, mind you. Cash."

I moved over to the bookcase, picked out a *Who's Who* and started running through the *B*'s.

Bertha narrowed blazing eyes at me for a moment, then moved to look over my shoulder. I could feel her hot, angry breath on my neck.

There was no John Carver Billings.

I reached for *Who's Who in California*. Bertha beat me to it, jerked the book out of the bookcase, and said, "Suppose *I* do the brain work for a while and you get out and case that motor court?"

"Okay," I told her, starting for the door, "only don't strain the equipment to a point of irreparable damage."

I thought for a moment she was going to throw the book.

She didn't.

Chapter Two

Elsie Brand, my secretary, looked up from her typing.

"A new case?"

I nodded.

"How's Bertha?"

"Her same old irascible, greedy, profane self. How would you like to act the part of a falling woman?"

"A fallen woman?"

"I said a *falling* woman."

"Oh, I see. Present participle. What do I do?"

I said, "You come with me while I register us in a motor court as husband and wife."

"And then what?" she asked cautiously.

"Then," I said, "we do detective work."

"Will I need any baggage?"

"I'll stop by my apartment and pick up a suitcase. That should be all we need."

Elsie walked over to the coat closet, got her hat, and pulled the cover down on her typewriter.

As we left the office I said, "You might be looking this over," and handed her the description of the two women which Bertha Cool had scrawled on the paper in her heavy-fisted writing.

Elsie studied the slip of paper on the way down in the elevator and said, "Evidently the man fell for Sylvia and hated Millie."

"How did you know?"

"Good Lord, listen," she said. " 'Sylvia, attractive brunette with dark, lustrous eyes; sympathetic, intelligent, beautiful, five feet two, weight a hundred and twelve, swell figure, around twenty-three or twenty-four, fine dancer. Millie, redheaded, blue-eyed, snippy, smart, may be twenty-five or twenty-six, average height, fair figure.' "

I grinned. "Well, we'll now try to find out how much information those women left behind in a motor court that's been occupied three times since they were there."

"Suppose the people who run it can tell us anything?"

"That's why I want you along," I said. "I want to find out whether it's a careful motor court or whether it isn't."

"Thanks for the compliment."

"Don't mention it," I told her.

I picked up the agency heap at the parking lot. We stopped at my apartment. Elsie sat in the car while I went up and threw a few things into a suitcase. As an afterthought I brought an overcoat along. There was a leather bag for cameras that could have been used by a woman, and I stuck that under my arm.

Elsie looked the collection over curiously. "Evidently," she said, "we're traveling light."

I nodded.

We went out Sepulveda and I drove along slowly, studying the motor courts. At this hour they all had signs in front announcing vacancies.

"That's the one we want," I said to Elsie. "The one over there on the right."

We turned in.

The doors were wide open on most of the units. A Negro maid was hauling out linen. A rather attractive girl wearing a cap and apron was also working around the place. It took five minutes to locate the manager.

She was a big woman about Bertha's build, except that where Bertha was as hard as a roll of barbed wire, this woman was soft, all except her eyes. They were Bertha's eyes.

"How about accommodations?" I asked.

She looked past me to where Elsie was sitting in the car trying to look virtuous.

"For how long?"

"All day and all night."

She showed surprise.

"My wife and I," I explained, "have been driving all night. We want a rest and then we want to look around the city and pull out early tomorrow morning."

"I have a nice single at five dollars."

"How about Cabin Number Five over there in the corner?"

"That's a double. You wouldn't want that."

"How much is it?"

"Eleven dollars."

"I'll take it."

"No, you won't."

I raised my eyebrows.

She said, "I don't think you'll take anything."

"Why not?"

She said, "Listen, I'm running a high-class place. If you know this girl well enough to go into a single cabin as man and wife and you have the money to pay for it, that's okay by me. If you're selling her on the idea that you're getting a double cabin I know what *that* means."

I said, "There won't be any noise, there won't be any rough stuff. You can have twenty bucks for Number Five. Is it a deal?"

She looked Elsie over. "Who is she?" she asked.

I said, "She's my secretary. I'm not going to make any passes. If I did, I wouldn't get rough. We're traveling on a business trip and—"

"Okay," she said. "Twenty bucks."

I handed her the twenty, got the key to the cabin, and drove the car into the garage.

We unlocked the door and walked in. It was a good-looking double cabin, with a little sitting-room and two bedrooms, each with a shower and toilet.

"You going to get any information out of her?" Elsie asked.

"I don't think so," I said. "If she knew anything she wouldn't tell. She isn't the type that gabs, and she doesn't want to have attention focused on the motor court."

"It's a nice place," Elsie said, walking around and looking it over. "Clean as a pin and the furniture's nice."

"Uh-huh," I said. "Now let's get busy and try and find something that will give us an idea as to the identity of two women who had this cabin three nights ago."

"Did I hear you say twenty dollars?" she asked.

"That's right. She didn't want to rent it at the regular price."

"Bertha will certainly scream over that when she sees it on the expense account."

I nodded, looking around the place.

"Isn't this something of a wild-goose chase?" she asked.

"It's all a wild-goose chase," I told her. "Let's start looking. We might even find the golden egg."

We prowled the place and found nothing except a couple of bobby pins. Then when I pulled a bureau drawer all the way out I found a piece of paper that had slipped into a crack in the back of the drawer.

"What's that?" Elsie asked.

I said, "That seems to be the gummed label that has slipped off a prescription box. It's a San Francisco prescription made to Miss Sylvia Tucker. It says, 'Take one capsule for sleeplessness. Do not repeat within four hours,' and it's a prescription that can't be refilled."

"With the name of a San Francisco drugstore on it," Elsie said.

"And," I pointed out, "a prescription number and the name of a doctor."

"And Sylvia from San Francisco is one of the women we want?"

"That's right."

"How fortunate," Elsie said.

"How very, very, very fortunate," I observed.

She looked at me.

"What do you mean by that?"

"I mean that it's very, very fortunate."

"Well, what about it? The girl was here. She gave John Billings a little shot of sleepy-by medicine. When she did, the label came off the box with the prescription number on it."

I said, "Sylvia was the girl he liked. It was the other one who gave him the by-by."

"That's what he thinks. John Carver Billings the Second may not be such a knockout as he thinks he is. Anyway, the other gal could have borrowed a capsule from Sylvia without her knowing it."

I stood there, studying the label.

"What do we do now?" Elsie asked.

"Now," I said, "we go back to the office. Then I take a plane to San Francisco."

"This *was* a short honeymoon," she told me. "Are you going to tell the manager she can have the apartment?"

"No. We'll keep her guessing," I said. "Come on, let's go."

I saw the puzzled eyes of the woman who managed the place looking at us as we drove out.

Back in the office I put through a phone call for a cor-respondent in San Francisco who checked with the drugstore and had the information for me within an hour and twenty minutes.

Sylvia Tucker lived in the Truckee Apartments out on Post Street. The apartment number was 608, and the prescription had been for sodium amytal. She was employed as a manicurist in a barbershop on Post Street.

Elsie got me a plane reservation and I stopped in to tell Bertha I was headed for San Francisco.

"How are you doing, Donald, lover?" she asked with her best cooing manner.

"As well as was expected."

"Well, what the hell does that mean? Are we going to get that five-hundred-dollar bonus?"

"Probably."

"Well, don't go running up a lot of expenses."

"He's paying them, isn't he?"

"Sure. But if it's going to be a long-drawn-out job, he'll—"

"It isn't going to be too long-drawn-out."

"Don't solve it *too* fast, Donald."

"That's why he offered the bonus. He didn't want us stalling in order to get more per diems."

"Who the hell said anything about stalling?"

"You didn't."

She glared at me.

"Did you look up John Carver Billings the First?"

"Now *that* was a swell idea of yours, Donald, dear," she said. "I have to hand it to you for that one. It gives us background."

"Who is he?"

"Some banking buzzard from San Francisco. President of half a dozen companies, fifty-two years old, a rich, eligible widower, commodore of a yachting club, lousy with dough. Does that mean anything to you?"

"It means a lot to me," I told her. "It means the son came by it honestly."

"The money?" she asked complacently.

"The sport coat," I told her.

Bertha's face darkened, then she laughed. "You have to have your smart crack, don't you, Donald? But just remember, lover, that it takes money to make the wheels go round."

"And while the wheels are going round and round," I warned her, "be careful you don't get a finger caught in the machinery."

"Fry me for an oyster," she blazed. "You'd think I was some simple, naïve amateur. You just keep your own nose clean, Donald Lam, and I'll take care of mine. When Bertha reaches for anything she gets what she reaches for. *You're* the one to be careful. You almost dropped a monkey wrench in those wheels that are now spinning around so nicely."

And Bertha's complacency puckered into a reproving frown.

"They're spinning around like crazy," I admitted. "Personally, I'd like to see what the machine is manufacturing."

"You can roast me for a duck," she snapped, "if you aren't the most gift-horse-in-the-mouth-looking bastard I ever saw. I'll tell you what the little wheels are manufacturing, Donald. It's money!"

And Bertha once more gloated over the page of *Who's Who in California*.

I eased out of the office and left her to her thoughts.

Chapter Three

It was late afternoon when I disembarked at the San Francisco airport. I got into the barbershop on Post Street just before it was closing.

It didn't take more than two seconds to pick out Sylvia. There were three manicurists in the place but Sylvia was the pick of the lot, and with the description I had of her it was like shooting fish in a barrel.

She was busy when I walked in, but when I asked her if she'd have time for one more before closing, she looked at the clock, nodded, and started making her fingers really fly over the nails of a big lug who glared at me resentfully.

I went over to the shoe-shining stand and let the boy work on my shoes while I was waiting.

The head barber came over to me. "You waiting for a manicure?"

"Right."

"There's a girl ready for you now."

"I want Sylvia."

"This other girl's just as good—in fact a little better than Sylvia."

"Thanks, I'll wait."

He went back to his chair.

"Sounds a little unfriendly to Sylvia," I told the bootblack.

He grinned, glanced cautiously over his shoulder, said, "She's sure in the doghouse."

"What's the matter?"

"They don't pay me to gossip."

"Perhaps they don't, but I will."

He thought that over, bent low over my shoes, said guardedly, "He's jealous. He's been making a big play for her. Tuesday she phoned she had a headache and couldn't work; then she never showed up again until this morning. He thinks she was out with a boyfriend. Don't think she's going to be here long."

I slid two dollars down to him. "Thanks," I said. "I was just curious, that's all."

The man Sylvia had been working on got up and put on his coat. Sylvia nodded to me. The boy finished my shoes, and I went over to Sylvia's table.

The head barber kept his face averted.

With one hand in the bowl of warm, soapy water, I sat relaxing, letting Sylvia's soft, competent fingers hold my other hand while she started filing my nails.

"Been here long?" I asked after a while.

"About a year."

"Get any vacations on this job?"

"Oh, yes. I just got back from a short vacation."

"Swell. Where'd you go?"

"Los Angeles."

"Alone?"

"Fresh!"

"I was just asking."

"I had a girlfriend with me. We had always wanted to take a look through Hollywood and see if we could see some of the movie stars in one of the night clubs."

"Did you?"

"No."

"What stopped you?"

"We went, but we didn't find the movie stars, that's all."

"There's quite a few of them around and they have to eat, you know."

"Not when we were eating, they didn't."

"How long were you there?"

"A couple of days. I just got back last night."

"Go on the train?"

"No. My girlfriend has a car."

I said, "This is Friday. Where were you Tuesday night?"

"That's the night we got into Hollywood."

"Suppose you tell me what happened Tuesday night."

"And suppose I don't?" she said, her eyes suddenly flashing.

I didn't say anything more.

She worked over my hands. The silence became oppressive.

"I'm over twenty-one and my own boss," she volunteered after a while. "I don't have to account for the things I do."

"Or the things you *don't* do?" I asked.

She looked at me sharply. "Where are you from?"

"Los Angeles."

"When did you get in?"

"Just now."

"How did you come?"

"By plane."

"What time did you arrive?"

"An hour ago."

"You must have got off the plane and come directly here."

"I did."

"Why were you interested in what happened Tuesday night in Los Angeles?"

"Just making conversation."

"Oh," she said.

I didn't say anything more.

She slowed down her pace and started marking time. Two or three times she looked at me curiously, started to say something, then caught herself and quit. After a while she said, "You up here on business?"

"Sort of."

"I suppose you know lots of people up here."

I shook my head.

"It must be lonesome to come into a strange town."

Again I nodded.

She suddenly put down her things and said, "My heavens, there's one phone call I have to make. I almost forgot it."

She dashed off to a phone booth; dialed a number, and talked for three or four minutes. Twice, she looked at me while she was talking, as though she were describing me over the phone.

Then she came back, sat down, and said, "Gosh, I hope you'll pardon me."

"Sure, it's all right. I don't have anything to do. Just so you're not kept here too late."

By that time the shop had closed up, the curtains had been pulled, and the barbers were getting ready to go home.

"Oh, that's all right," she told me. "I'm not in a hurry any longer. That phone call—My dinner date blew up."

"Too bad," I told her.

She worked in silence for a while longer, then said, "Darned if it wasn't. I had my heart all set on going out to dinner and there isn't a thing to eat in my apartment."

"Why not go out with me?"

"Oh, I'd love to. I—Well, now, wait a minute. There's a lot about you I don't know."

"The name," I said, "is Donald. Donald Lam."

"I'm Sylvia Tucker."

"Hello, Sylvia."

"Hello, Donald. Are you nice?"

"I try to be."

"I'm not a gold digger, but I like thick and juicy steaks and I know where to get them. They come high."

"That's okay."

"I wouldn't want you to get any funny ideas."

"I haven't."

"After all, you know, this is— Well, you must think it's an easy pickup."

"I hadn't thought of it as being a pickup," I said. "I have to eat somewhere, you have to eat somewhere. Why be lonely?"

"That's a nice way of looking at it. I think you're a square shooter."

"I try to be."

She said, "Ordinarily I don't pick up. I just have a few friends, but— Well, I don't know, you're different, somehow. You don't seem to be on the make the way most of them are."

"Is *that* a compliment?"

"Oh, I didn't mean it that way. You're not— Oh, you know what I meant." She laughed. "I bet you have a terrific line, but— Well, what I meant was that you weren't like so many of them. You don't take it for granted that a girl will date just because she happens to be working at a job of this kind."

I didn't say anything.

She worked in silence for a while, then said, "I certainly had one funny experience on the last pickup."

"Yes?"

"Uh-huh," she said brightly. "My girlfriend was with me and the fellow was certainly amorous. I had some sleeping-medicine the doctor had given me, and without my knowing anything about it she slipped one of the capsules in his drink. He went out like a light."

"Why did your girlfriend do that? Didn't she like the guy? Or did she feel that your virtue had to be protected at all hazards?"

"Not at *all* hazards," she said, flashing me a provocative glance. "I guess Millie just did it for—a lot of devilment. She's a funny girl; a cute little redhead. And I don't know, perhaps she was a little peeved this fellow wasn't falling for her. You never can tell about women. He was a nice boy, too."

"Then what happened?"

"Oh, nothing. I just mentioned it."

I said, "Uh-huh," and kept quiet.

She finished with my hands, doing a lot of thinking.

"I'll have to run up to my apartment," she said.

"Okay. You want me to come along or shall I pick you up there later?"

"Why don't you come on up?"

"Promise you won't give me any sleeping-pills?"

"I'll promise." She laughed. "Millie won't be there. She's the one that did the dirty work."

"Must have been quite a joke."

"It was. I was half mad at the time because I liked this boy, but honestly, Donald, it certainly *was* funny!

"He was very much the man about town and the daddy of the party. He was just beginning to get really interested in me when this drink took effect. Then he started to make me a proposition in a sleepy sort of a way and went by-by right in the middle of it.

"Millie and I put him to bed on the couch and he was dead to the world until morning when we wakened him for breakfast. You should have *seen* the expression on his face when he woke up and realized the night and the opportunity had both completely passed."

She threw back her head and laughed.

"I'll bet it was funny," I said. "Where did all this take place?"

"In an auto court. Millie is never one to overlook a golden opportunity. She asked this fellow about where the good auto courts were, so of course he volunteered to take us out and show us, and that meant he registered, and *that* meant he paid the money."

"Well, at least he got a good night's sleep for his investment," I commented.

That made her laugh again. "Come on, Donald. I'll take you up to my apartment and buy you a drink. Then we'll go out."

"Do we walk or take a cab?"

"It's about six blocks," she said.

"We take a cab," I told her.

We walked out to the curb. "While we're waiting for a cab," I asked casually, "where was this court?"

"Out on Sepulveda."

"When was all this?"

"Why, let's see— Why, Donald, that was Tuesday night."

"Are you sure?"

"Why, of course. Why, what difference would it make?"

"Oh, I don't know. I was just wondering about your vacation."

"Well, that's the way it was."

A taxi pulled in to the curb. Sylvia gave him the address and we settled back in the cushions. At that time of night running six blocks involved a lot of stopping and starting.

"The three of you in the one cabin?"

"Uh-huh. It was a nice double cabin."

"You had one room, Millie had the other, and you parked this boy on the couch?"

"That's right. Sort of a davenport."

"Wouldn't that make up into a bed also? That's usually the way in those motor courts."

"Oh, I guess so, but we didn't bother. We just parked him, took his shoes off, and I donated a pillow from my bed."

"Any blankets?"

"Don't be silly! We put his overcoat over his feet and locked our doors. If he woke up and got cold he could call a taxi and go home."

"Where," I asked, "do *we* eat?"

She said, "I know a nice restaurant. It's out a ways, but—"

"That's all right," I told her. "Only I have a reservation on the ten o'clock plane."

"Tonight, Donald?" she asked, with keen disappointment in her voice.

I nodded.

She snuggled over close to me and slipped her hand into mine.

"Oh, well," she said. "You'll have plenty of time—to eat and catch your plane."

Chapter Four

Elsie Brand poked her head into my private office and said, "Bertha has the client in her office. He's asking if there's anything new."

"Tell Bertha I'll be right in."

She looked at me curiously. "Do any good in San Francisco last night?"

"Quite a bit."

"Nice trip?"

"Uh-huh."

"Find Sylvia?"

"Yes."

"How was she?"

"Up to specifications."

"Oh."

Elsie Brand retired to her office and pulled the door shut.

I waited for a few minutes, then went into Bertha Cool's office.

John Carver Billings the Second seemed to be somewhat excited. He was sitting erect in the chair, smoking a cigarette.

Bertha's eyes glittered as she looked at me. "Are you getting anywhere?"

I said, "The name of the girl who was in the motor court is Sylvia Tucker. She's employed as a manicurist in a Post Street barbershop in San Francisco. She has an apartment about six blocks from where she works. She's a cute babe. She remembers the occasion perfectly and is about half sore at her girlfriend for slipping the sodium amytal in Billings's drink."

"Do you mean you've found her? You've got all that information?" Billings exclaimed, jumping up out of the chair.

"Uh-huh."

Bertha beamed at me. "Fry me for an oyster!" she said affectionately.

"Well, now *that's* what I call darn good detective work," Billings said. "You're sure this is the girl?"

I said, "She told me all about going to Los Angeles on a vacation. How she and her friend, Millie, went out to try and track down some famous movie stars at a night club, how they met you and Millie got you to 'recommend' a motor court, and then let you register so you'd be stuck with the bill.

"Sylvia had really fallen for you and was a little bit peeved when Millie put the sleeping-medicine in your drink, terminating the romantic possibilities and destroying your wolfish tendencies for the balance of the night."

"She told you all that?"

"All of it."

John Carver Billings the Second jumped up and grabbed my hand, pumping my arm up and down. He clapped me on the back, turned to Bertha, and said, "Now, that's the kind of work I like! That's *real* detective work!"

Bertha unscrewed the cap, and handed him her fountain pen.

"I don't get it," he said. "What? Oh."

He laughed, sat down, and made out a check for five hundred dollars.

Bertha beamed as though she wanted to kiss both of us.

I handed Carver a neatly typed report. "This tells how we found Sylvia Tucker," I said, "what her story is, where she works, and her home address. It also has the story she told me about what happened last Tuesday evening. You can get her to make an affidavit if it's important."

"You didn't ask her about making an affidavit, did you?"

"No, I just got the information. I didn't even let her know that I was trying to get that information. I just drew it out of her."

"That's swell. I'm glad you didn't tell her it was important."

"We figure our job is to get information, not to give it."

"Capital!" he exclaimed. "Lam, you're all right. That's fine."

He folded the report, put it in the pocket of his sport coat, shook hands once more all around, and walked out.

Bertha beamed at me. "You're crazy as a loon," she said. "And sometimes I could kill you, but you sure as hell do bring home the bacon."

"Uh-huh."

"That was fast work, Donald, lover. How did you do it?"

I said, "I followed the paper trail."

"What do you mean, the paper trail?"

"I followed the clues that had very carefully been left for me to follow."

Bertha started to say something, then suddenly blinked her hard little glittering eyes and said, "Say that again, Donald."

I said, "I followed the clues that had been carefully left

for me to follow."

"What the hell do you mean by that?"

"Just what I said."

"Who left the clues?"

I shrugged my shoulders.

"Are you trying to get temperamental with me now?"

"No, not at all," I said, "but why not think it out for yourself?"

"How come?"

I said, "Well, take the story of John Carver Billings the Second. You'll remember he told about picking up these two girls who had just arrived in Hollywood on their vacation."

"Yes."

I said, "That was Tuesday night. He came to see us yesterday. Today is Saturday."

"Well?"

"I found a label off a prescription box in the drawer in the motor court. I went to San Francisco and called on the girl. She said she'd just got back the night before and had gone to work yesterday morning."

"Well, what's wrong with that?"

I said, "According to her story they left San Francisco Monday evening at five o'clock. They drove as far as Salinas, stayed there that night, then drove down to Hollywood the next day. They went directly to a cocktail parlor. Billings picked them up. They went to the motor court. That was Tuesday night. They checked out Wednesday morning and went to another motor court. They were there Wednesday night. Then, early Thursday morning, they left to return to San Francisco. They got to San Francisco late Thursday night and the girls started working again yesterday."

"So what?"

"Hell of a vacation, wasn't it?"

Bertha said, "Lots of people have to take short vacations. They can't get away for longer periods."

"Sure," I said.

"Well, what's wrong with that?" Bertha demanded.

I said, "Suppose you had four days that you could take as a vacation, and you wanted to go to Los Angeles; what would you do?"

"I'd go to Los Angeles," Bertha said. "Dammit, come to the point."

I said, "You'd arrange your vacation so it started on Monday or so it ended on Saturday, or both. You'd leave on Saturday morning—or Saturday noon—if you had to work Saturday morning. You'd have all Saturday afternoon and Sunday added to your vacation. You wouldn't work Monday, then leave Monday night and get back Thursday night so you could go to work Friday."

Bertha thought that over. "Slice me for an onion," she said, half to herself.

"Moreover," I said, "as soon as this girl had me spotted as a detective who was trying to pump her about that particular trip, I quit talking about it and pretended I wasn't going to do any more talking. For a minute she got in a panic, being afraid she wasn't going to collect the bonus that had been guaranteed to her for handing me that story. She must have thought I was a hell of a detective. She damn near had to ask me to take her out to dinner. She almost dragged me up to her apartment. She fell all over herself seeing that I got the proper information."

"Well, you got it," Bertha said, "and we got the money. What is there for us to worry about?"

"I hate to be played for a sucker."

"We got three hundred bucks out of that bird when he came in yesterday morning. We got five hundred bucks out of him this morning. That's eight hundred dollars for a two-day case. And if they want to play Big Bertha for a sucker to the tune of four hundred bucks a day they can move right in."

Bertha banged her jeweled hand down on the desk by way of emphasis.

"Okay by me," I told her, got up and started for the door.

"Say," Bertha said, as I had my hand on the knob, "do you suppose that whole damned alibi is faked, Donald?"

I shrugged my shoulders. "You've got the money. What more do you want?"

Bertha said, "Wait a minute, lover. This may not be so good."

I said, "What's wrong about it?"

"If there's anything phony about it, that bastard paid out eight hundred dollars just for the privilege of having us fronting for an alibi that could be phony as hell."

"Well," I told her, "you said you didn't mind being played for a sucker at four hundred dollars a day. You'd better put two hundred dollars into a sinking fund."

"What for?"

"To buy a bail bond with," I said, and went out.

Chapter Five

I turned my car into the driveway on the Sepulveda Motor Court.

The manager looked up as I entered the office. Her eyes became angry. "What kind of a shenanigan were you trying to work on me?"

"Nothing," I said.

She said, "You rent a double cottage and are in there for about fifteen minutes. If it was going to be something like that, why didn't you have the decency to at least tell me when you were pulling out so I could have rented the apartment last night?"

"I didn't want you to rent it. I paid you enough for it, didn't I?"

"That's neither here nor there. If you weren't going to use it—"

I said, "Let's quit beating around the bush and suppose you tell me what you know about the people who were in there Tuesday night."

"Suppose I don't. I don't discuss my guests."

"It *might* save you some unpleasant publicity."

She looked up at me and then said, thoughtfully, "So that's what it is. It's a wonder I didn't realize it before."

"That's what it is."

"What do you want?"

"I want to see the registration for Tuesday night, and I want to talk with you."

"Is this the law?"

I shook my head.

She started drawing a red, lacquered fingernail across a sheet of letter paper on the desk, then carefully studying the indentation marks the nail had made. Apparently that was the most absorbing thing to do that she had found all day.

I stood there and waited.

Abruptly, she looked up. "Private?"

I nodded.

"What are you after?"

"I want to know who stayed there Tuesday."

"Why?"

I smiled at her.

She said, "I don't give out information like that. Running an auto court is a business in itself."

"Sure it is."

"I'd have to know why you wanted to know."

I said, "My business is confidential, too."

"Yes, I suppose so."

She went back to tracing patterns with the point of her

fingernail over the paper.

Abruptly she asked, "Could you keep me out of it?"

I said, "You live here. We live here. I wouldn't come out to see you this way if I was going to give you a double cross. I'd get the information some other way."

"How?"

"Having a friendly newspaper reporter or police officer come out."

She said, "I wouldn't like that."

"I didn't think you would."

She opened a drawer in the desk, reached in, and after a moment's search pulled out a card.

It was a registration card. It showed that the cabin had been rented Tuesday night to Ferguson L. Hoy and party, 551 Prince Street, Oakland, and the rental had been thirteen dollars.

I took a small copying camera from my briefcase, set it up on a tripod, turned on an electric light so there would be good illumination, and took a couple of pictures.

"That all?" she asked.

I shook my head. "Now I want to know something about Mr. Hoy."

She said, "I can't help you much there. He was just another man, as far as I'm concerned."

"Young?"

"I wouldn't remember. Come to think of it, it was one of the women with him who came in. She got a registration card and took it out to him. He was in the car. He signed it and sent back the thirteen dollars in exact change."

"How many people in the party?"

"Four—two couples."

"You didn't see this man well enough to remember him if you saw him again?"

"That's hard to say. I don't think so."

I said, "I was out here yesterday about eleven o'clock."

She nodded.

I said, "Someone had been in that cabin shortly before I arrived there."

She shook her head. "That cabin had all been cleaned up and—"

"Someone had been in there shortly before I arrived," I interrupted.

"I don't think so."

"Someone who was smoking a cigarette," I said.

She shook her head.

"Do the maids smoke?"

"No."

I said, "There were cigarette ashes on the top of the dresser; just a few that had spilled there."

"I don't think— Well, I don't know. The maids are supposed to wipe off the tops of the dressers when they clean up."

"I think this had been wiped. The cabin was slick as a pin."

I took my billfold from my pocket and held it so she could see it.

"Let's get one of the maids," I said.

The manager stepped to the door of the office. "They're down there at the far end. I don't want to go away where I can't hear the telephone. If you want to go down to the far end you might ask one of them to step in here. I'd like to have you question her in front of me. We can take them one at a time."

"Okay by me," I told her.

I walked out. She started to move even before I was out of the door.

The colored maid was a good-looking, intelligent young woman who seemed to have a good deal of savvy.

"The manager wants to see you," I told her.

She gave me a searching look and said, "What's the matter? Is something missing?"

"She didn't tell me. Just that she wanted to see you."

"You aren't accusing me of anything?"

I shook my head.

"You were here yesterday in Number Five?"

"That's right, I was," I told her. "And there's no complaint, but the manager would like to talk to you for a minute."

I turned and started to the manager's office and after a moment the girl followed me.

"Florence," the manager said, when she entered the room, "was anyone in the cabin before this man was in there yesterday? Number Five?"

"No, ma'am."

"You're sure?"

"Yes, ma'am."

I sat over on a corner of the desk and let one hand move over as though searching for something I could hold on to as a brace. The telephone was there. I let my fingers close around the receiver. It was still warm. The manager had telephoned someone while I'd been down at the far end of the court.

I said to the maid, "Wait a minute. I don't mean someone who stayed there. I mean someone who came in just for a minute, probably someone who said he'd forgotten something and—"

"Oh," she said, "that was the gentleman who stayed there Wednesday night. He'd forgotten something. He wouldn't tell me what it was. Just said to let him in and he'd get it. I told him I didn't think there was anything in there, but he handed me five dollars and— Lord, I hope I didn't do anything wrong."

"That's all right," I told her. "Now, I want you to

describe him. Was he a tall drink of water, about twenty-five or twenty-six, wearing a sport coat and slacks? He—"

"Lord, no," she interrupted. "This gentleman was wearin' a leather coat and a cap with lots of gold braid."

"Military?" I asked.

"Like the swells on yachts," she said. "But he sure was tall and string-bean-like."

"He gave you five dollars?"

"That's right."

I gave her five dollars and said, "There's the mate to it. How long was he in there?"

"He wasn't in there more'n long enough to just turn around and come back. I heard a couple of drawers opening and closing and then he was right out all covered with grins. I asked him if he'd found what he'd lost and he laughed and said after he got in there he remembered he'd put it in the pocket of his other suit and packed his suit in the suitcase. He said he was kind of absent-minded, and jumped in his car and drove off."

"Do you know he stayed there in that cabin Wednesday night?"

"Of course not. I go off work at four-thirty in the afternoon. But he *said* he'd stayed there Wednesday."

The manager looked at me. "Anything else?"

I turned to the maid. "You'd know this man if you saw him again?"

"I'll tell the world I'd know him, just like I'd know you. Five-dollar tips don't grow on bushes on this job."

I went back to the agency heap, drove to the nearest pay station, telephoned Elsie Brand, and said, "Elsie, I won't be around for the weekend. I'm going to be in San Francisco. Tell Bertha, in case she wants to know, that whatever we're working on is going to be in San Francisco."

"Why?" she asked.

I said, "Because a six-foot string bean with a yachtsman's cap has been down here in our honeymoon cottage."

"*Some* honeymoon," she retorted. "Give Sylvia my love."

Chapter Six

Millicent Rhodes was engraved on a strip of cardboard which had been neatly cut from a visiting-card and inserted in the holder opposite the push button on Millie's apartment out on Geary Street.

I pressed the bell button.

Nothing happened.

I pressed it again for a long ring, then three short rings.

The speaking-tube made noise. A girl's voice said protestingly, "It's Saturday morning. Go away."

"I have to see you," I said. "And it isn't morning. It's afternoon."

"Who are you?"

"A friend of Sylvia's—Donald Lam."

She didn't give assent specifically, but after a second or two the electric buzzer on the door signified that she had pushed the button which unlatched the door for me.

Millicent had apartment 342. The elevator was at the far end of the hall, but, since the oblong of light showed the cage was waiting at the ground floor, I walked back to it. It took the swaying, wheezy cage almost as long to get to the third floor as it would have taken me to walk up the stairs.

Millie Rhodes opened the door almost as soon as my finger touched the button.

"I hope this is important," she said coldly.

"It is."

"All right, come in. This is Saturday. I don't have to work so I take it easy. It's probably the one symbol of economic freedom I can afford."

I looked at her in surprise.

She was a good-looking, well-formed redhead, despite the fact that there was no make-up on her face or lips. She had evidently tumbled out of bed in response to my ring and had simply thrown a silk wrap around her to answer the door. It was quite apparent she was easy on the eyes despite the attire.

"You're different from the description I had of you," I said.

She made a little grimace. "Give a girl a break. Let me get some make-up on and some clothes and—"

"I meant it the other way."

"What other way?"

"You're a lot more attractive than the description."

"I guess I'll have to speak to Sylvia," she said grimly.

"Not Sylvia," I told her. "Someone else. I gathered you were a demon chaperon."

She looked at me with a puzzled frown for a moment, then said, "I don't get it. Find yourself a chair and sit down. You've caught me pretty much unawares, but any friend of Sylvia's is a friend of mine."

"I waited as late as I could," I said. "I was hoping you'd be up and I wouldn't have to disturb you."

"Skip it. It's done now. Anyhow, I'm not working this week. The Saturday sleep is just a deeply entrenched habit."

She looked as though she needed a cigarette. I offered her one, and she took it eagerly. She tapped the end of it gently on the edge of a little table, leaned forward for my light, settled back on the edge of the bed, then, after a moment, propped her back up with pillows, kicked her feet up, and said, "I suppose I *should* have kept you waiting while I made the bed, put it up out of sight, and spread the chairs around, but I decided you could take me as I am. Now, what about Sylvia?"

I said, "Sylvia told me an interesting story."

"Sometimes she does."

"I wanted it verified."

"If Sylvia told it to you, it's verified."

I said, "It involves a trip you took to Hollywood, a short vacation trip."

She suddenly threw back her head and laughed. "*Now* I get it," she said, "the demon-chaperon part. I suppose Sylvia will never forgive me for it, but she was feeling her drinks and feeling romantic, and she started to fall for this fellow. There was no percentage in it—for Sylvia, that is. I slipped him a nightcap with some sleeping-medicine in it. You should have seen him trying to be passionate one minute and drowsy the next. I thought I'd laugh right in his face."

"I understand he finally passed out."

"Like a light. We parked him on the davenport, covered him up, tucked him in, and sought our virtuous couches."

"I trust you made him comfortable."

"Oh, sure."

I said, "Sylvia said you took his shoes off. Sylvia made the davenport into a bed, and then you tucked him in."

She hesitated a moment, then said, "That's right."

"You put his shoes under the bed, hung his coat over the back of a chair, and left him with his pants on."

"That's right."

"A warm night?"

"Fairly warm. We covered him."

"You don't know his name?"

"Heavens, no. Not his last name. We called him John. You said your name was Donald?"

"That's right."

"Well, why talk so much about what happened down there in Los Angeles, Donald? What do you want?"

"To talk about what happened in Los Angeles."

"Why?"

"I'm a detective."

"A what?"

"A detective."

"You don't look it."

"Private," I said.

"Say, maybe I'm talking too much."

"Not enough."

"How long have you known Sylvia? I don't remember hearing her speak of you."

"I met her yesterday afternoon, and went to dinner with her."

"That's the first time you met her?"

"That's right."

"Say, what are you getting at, anyway? What are you after?"

"Information."

"Well," she said, "I guess you've got it, and your gain is my loss."

"How do you mean?"

"My beauty sleep. For whom are you working?"

"The man who was with you."

"Don't be silly. He doesn't know who we are. He couldn't find us in a hundred years. We checked out of the motor court the next morning so he couldn't. I was afraid he might get suspicious and resentful."

"No," I said. "He hired me. I found you."

"How?"

"Simple enough. You used sleeping-capsules that a doctor had given Sylvia on a prescription. The gummed label fell off the box and was caught in the back of one of the bureau drawers."

"Say," she said, "you might be right at that!"

"It had slipped down behind one of the drawers in the bureau."

She made a little gesture of disgust. "I thought I was being a smart girl. I suppose I *could* have got into trouble over that deal. What's this guy going to think? Does he know he was drugged?"

I nodded. "He figured you'd pulled a fast one on him."

"Before the label was found or afterward?"

"Before."

"He wasn't such a bad sort, only he was a little too obvious and impulsive. I guess he has money. That's probably half the trouble with him. He feels that just because he buys a girl a good dinner and a few drinks he has the right to move right in and share her life."

I didn't say anything.

"Who is he, Donald?"

I said, "Suppose you tell *me* what *you* know about him."

"Any reason why I should?"

"No. Any reason why you shouldn't?"

She hesitated a moment, looking at me from under long lashes and said, "You seem to cut your cake in big pieces."

"Why do things halfway?" I asked.

She laughed. "I guess you don't have to."

I remained silent.

She said, "Sylvia and I were on the prowl. Sylvia is more impulsive than I am. This fellow was on the make. We needed an escort and we needed someone to pay the check. We—"

"Don't, Millie," I said.

"Don't what?"

"Don't go on with that line."

"I thought you wanted to know."

I said, "You're an intelligent girl and you're a good-looking girl. There's no percentage with that line. It won't work. How much is Billings paying you?"

"What do you mean?"

I said, "You've overlooked a lot of little things. I just wanted to make certain that you knew him before I called them to your attention."

"What do you mean?"

I said, "If you'd been really adept at the game you'd have insisted I talk with the two of you together. Letting me get you one at a time was a fatal weakness, and shows how amateurish you are."

"You're doing the talking now," she said, her greenish-blue eyes hard, wary, and watchful.

"According to Sylvia, he was placed on the couch fully clothed, with only a pillow behind his head. The davenport wasn't made up into a bed, there were no blankets for him. Sylvia donated a pillow and that was all."

She hesitated a moment, then said, "Give me another cigarette, Donald."

I gave her one.

She said, "I could try to juggle this one but I know it wouldn't do any good. Sylvia phoned me you'd swallowed it hook, line, and sinker. You were young, gullible, and a pushover for a girl who had good-looking legs."

"I am," I told her.

She laughed.

"Come on," she said, after a short silence. "How did you get wise?"

"You mean how much do I know?"

"I'm feeling my way," she said.

"There were certain things about the story that gave it every appearance of being synthetic," I told her. "How long have you known John Billings?"

"I just met him. He's one of Sylvia's friends."

"You don't know *all* of her friends?"

"Not the ones that have money," she said, and laughed. "Sylvia plays some things close to her chest."

"How much did he pay you?"

"Two hundred and fifty bucks. That is, Sylvia passed it over. She said that was my share of the take."

"Exactly what did she say you were to do in return?"

"She said I could get two hundred and fifty dollars if I was willing to have my picture in a newspaper. She said I'd have to play the part of a fallen woman, but she thought I could be 'fallen' in name only."

"What did you tell her?"

"You're here, aren't you?"

"Yes."

"Well, that's the answer."

"And then you met Billings?"

"Just over cocktails. He passed over the money and took a look at me so he'd know me when he saw me, and I took a look at him so I could identify him, and we had a drink or two, then he and Sylvia went out."

"Who fixed up the story?"

"Sylvia."

"Why does he want an alibi? Do you know?"

"No."

"You mean that you didn't ask?"

"There were five nice, crisp fifty-dollar bank notes. I wouldn't have asked a question of any one, let alone the whole five."

"How much did he pay Sylvia? Do you know?"

"He and Sylvia are—" She held up her hand with the first and second fingers crossed.

I said, "I'm sorry I disturbed you."

"Don't mention it. It was all part of the two hundred and fifty bucks. I rather expected you last night but Sylvia telephoned you had to go back to Los Angeles."

I nodded.

"You must be wearing out airplanes."

"I'm moving around."

"Now what do I do?"

"Keep quiet."

"Do I ring Sylvia and tell her that you were wise all along, that you trapped me and—"

"Then what would Sylvia do?"

"Oh," she said, "Sylvia would blame it all on me. She'd swear she'd pulled the wool over your eyes and everything was fine until you came to talk with me, and then I let the cat out of the bag. That's all right; you couldn't expect Sylvia to take any responsibility, not with it being one of *her* boyfriends."

"How many does she have?"

"Two or three."

"How many do you have?"

"None of your business."

"A lot of things are going to be my business. How many do you have?"

She looked at me and said, "None. Not in the way that you mean."

I said, "That's the answer that I expected."

"It happens to be true."

"I think it is," I told her and got up from the chair. "Can you tell me why Sylvia happened to pick on you to back up her story?"

"Because we're friends."

"Any other reason?"

"And I was available."

"Meaning what?"

"That I happened to be taking a week of my vacation. That meant no one could check on me and find I'd been at work when I said I'd been in Los Angeles.

"I guess Sylvia would rather have had one of her other friends. We're not *too* close. But the vacation business got me the two-fifty. Nice business, isn't it? Once you can get it. Tell me, Donald, am I in bad?"

"Not with me."

"With anyone?"

"Not yet."

"But I shouldn't stick with the story?"

"I wouldn't."

"Where are you going now?"

"To work."

"Can't I fix you a cup of coffee?"

I shook my head.

"And you're not going to tell Sylvia I spilled the beans?"

"No."

"What do *I* tell her?"

"Tell her I showed up and asked you questions."

"And that's all?"

"That's all."

She said, "You're letting me off pretty easy, aren't you, Donald?"

"I'm trying to."

She said, "Thanks. I'll remember it."

I closed the door, walked down the two flights of steps, and went to police headquarters.

I picked a man who looked as though he might be able to do me some good, got acquainted, showed him my credentials, said, "I want information. It's information that's a matter of public record but I want to get it fast. I'm going to need a little help. I'm willing to pay for it."

I took out a ten-dollar bill.

"What's the information?"

"I want to get a list of hit-and-run driving accidents on last Tuesday night."

"Just hit-and-run?"

"I'd like the whole crime list—but hit-and-run particularly."

"Can you give me the location?"

"Just anywhere around this part of the country."

He said, "Why the hit-and-run? You got a hunch?"

I shook my head. "I haven't a thing that will be of any help to you. I don't even know it's hit-and-run, but judging from the type of man I'm dealing with I think it *might* be hit-and-run. That looks like the most obvious explanation."

"Explanation for what?"

"Explanation for why I gave you ten bucks to dig up the information for me."

He said, "Sit right here, buddy. I'll be back."

I sat there and cussed myself for having associated with Bertha so long I was picking up her ways. Fifty dollars would have done the job. Ten bucks wasn't enough. However, I'd heard Bertha scream so much about expenses that I'd unconsciously begun to start economizing. I decided in the future to play things *my* way. A cop who is willing to take anything on the side is apt to regard ten dollars the same way a bellboy looks at a ten-cent tip.

My man was back, however, in about ten minutes with the information I wanted.

"Two cases are the only ones you could be interested in, buddy. A man was hit at Post and Polk by a car driven by a young fellow who was probably drunk. A jane was sitting next to the driver, and, according to spectators, had amalgamated herself pretty thoroughly with him. She was crawling all over him. He was driving pretty fast. He hit this pedestrian, broke a hip, an ankle, and a shoulder, knocked the guy over to the curb, slowed for a stop, then evidently remembered how many drinks he'd had and went away from there fast. He got a break. No one seems to have taken his license number. It happened pretty fast, you know. A car behind him, halfway down the block, saw the whole thing and took after the hit-and-run. He had good ideas but his execution wasn't so hot.

"Another car was just pulling out from the curb. They tangled. There was a smashing of fenders and cracking of glass. The road was blocked, no other cars could get through."

"Any physical clues?" I asked.

"I told you the guy was lucky. The second accident took place right close to where the pedestrian had been hit. We've got quite a few assorted pieces of glass and some bits from a broken grill. So far, the assorted junk all came from one or the other of the cars that were in the collision. The car that hit the pedestrian doesn't seem to have shed anything. If it did, it was mixed up with other stuff."

I nodded. "What was the other case?"

"The other case I don't think you're going to be interested in. A man was driving a car and was pretty drunk. He's out on bail."

I got up and said, "Well, I guess that does it."

He grinned at me and said, "The hell it does."

"What do you mean by that?"

"You've got a date with the man who's working on the case."

"When?"

"Now."

I said, "I don't know a thing. I'm here to get information. I—"

He said, "You tell it to the lieutenant."

"And furthermore," I went on, "if I had any information I wouldn't give it to the lieutenant or anybody else. I'm protecting a client."

"That's what you think."

I said, "When I protect a client I go all the way."

"You've gone all the way now, buddy. You've gone from Los Angeles to San Francisco. Try and protect a Los Angeles client up here and see where it gets you."

I said, "Try and beat information out of me and see where it gets *you*."

"We won't beat it out of you," he said, grinning. "We just shake it out of you."

He put a hand on my shoulder, a hand that was big as a ham, with strong fingers that slid down my arm until they took a grip on my elbow. "Right this way," he said.

Chapter Seven

Lieutenant Sheldon was a tall, slender individual who didn't look like a cop at all. He was wearing plain clothes and he sat behind a desk, assuming the attitude of a father-confessor. He stood up, shook hands, and said, "I'm *very* glad to meet you, Donald. Anything we can do for you up here we'll be only too glad to do."

"Thanks."

"We like to help the visiting firemen in every way we can."

"I'm sure I appreciate it."

"In return we expect a reasonable amount of co-opera-tion."

"Sure."

"You're interested in hit-and-run cases on Tuesday night?"

"Not exclusively. I was interested in the whole crime blotter, but I was giving special attention to hit-and-run."

"I know, I know," he said. "You wanted the whole thing. I've had it all typed out for you, Lam. Here it is."

He handed me a three-page list of crimes that included one case of molestation, three stickups, five burglaries, three driving while intoxicated. The list went on with solicitation, prostitution, gambling, and a charge of obtaining money under false pretenses.

I didn't get to read it all. Lieutenant Sheldon started talking. "Fold it and put it in your pocket, Lam. You'll have an opportunity to study it at your leisure. What do you know about the hit-and-run charge?"

"Nothing."

"You have a client, perhaps, who has an automobile that's been smashed up a little. You're a shrewd operator. You want to know just what you're getting into before you represent him, don't you?"

"No."

"You should."

"I mean I don't have a client who has a broken-up auto-mobile."

"Tut-tut," Lieutenant Sheldon said. "Let's not spar around with each other, Donald."

"I'm not sparring."

His eyes twinkled. "And don't try to get hardboiled. It doesn't buy you anything—up here."

"I'm satisfied it wouldn't."

"That's fine," he said. "So now we understand each other perfectly."

I nodded. "If I knew anything that would help on that hit-and-run charge I'd let you fellows know."

"Of course you would," Lieutenant Sheldon said. "I know you would. In the first place, we'd be very grateful for any co-operation, and in the second we'd be very, very much put out if we *didn't* get the co-operation."

I nodded.

"Now, the way I see it," Sheldon went on, "is that you're from Los Angeles. You have a detective agency down there and somebody came to you and said, 'Look, Lam, I had a little trouble when I was up in San Francisco. I had a few drinks and I had this girl along with me and she was getting affectionate and demonstrative, and there was a crowded street corner and I heard somebody yell. I don't *think* I hit anybody, but I'd just like to have you find out. And if I did hit anybody, you try to square it for me, will you?' "

I shook my head. "It isn't like that at all."

"I know," Sheldon said. "I'm just telling you the way I thought it *might* be."

I didn't say anything.

"So you come up here and start looking around to try and find out about what happened. Now that's all right as far as *you're* concerned, but as far as the department is concerned we'd like to have the credit of cleaning up the case and solving it. You understand that, don't you?"

I nodded.

Sheldon's eyes got hard. "So," he said, "if you know anything about it, you tell us and we'll all co-operate and play palsy-walsy; but if you don't co-operate, Donald, your man will be in one hell of a fix. There won't be anything he *can* square. He'll have the book thrown at him, and whenever you come to San Francisco you'll wish you'd stayed home." Again I nodded.

"So," Sheldon went on, "now that we've become acquainted, what have you got to tell us?"

"Nothing, yet."

"Now, we don't like that, Donald, I don't like the 'yet' and I don't like the 'nothing.' "

I didn't say anything.

He said, "You're going to want some co-operation at this end before you get done. Now's the time to lay the foundation for it."

I said, "You *could* be all cockeyed in your surmises."

"Of course I could, of course I could, Donald! You don't need to tell me that. Good heavens, some man could have walked into your office and said, 'Look, Donald, my boy went up to San Francisco and when he came home I'm satisfied he'd been in trouble of some sort. Now, he's a good boy but he does have a tendency to hoist a couple and then go out and get behind a steering wheel. Now, suppose you just slide up to San Francisco and see if there's any hit-and-run charge up there that hasn't been accounted for.'

"Or," Lieutenant Sheldon went on, "some man might have come to you and said, 'I saw a hit-and-run job up there in San Francisco. I was out with a woman who wasn't my wife and I simply can't afford to get mixed into it, but I'll give you a little information about what I saw and perhaps you can use it to locate the driver of the car and he'll take care of me in some way.' It could be any one of a hundred and one things."

I said, "I have a client. I haven't the faintest idea whether he knows anything about hit-and-run or not, but I'm interested in finding out. When I go back to Los Angeles I'm going to see that client. I'm going to put it up to him. If he was mixed up in any hit-and-run he's going to try and square it, and if he tries to square it he's going to come to you first. Now, how's that?"

Lieutenant Sheldon got up, came around the desk, grabbed my hand, and pumped it up and down. "Now, Donald," he said, "you're beginning to understand how we work in San Francisco; the way we try to co-operate with you fellows when you're up here. You don't try to do any squaring on the side. You pick up the telephone and you call for Lieutenant Sheldon, person to person. You get it?"

"I get it," I said.

"You tell me what you have, and you tell me what you want to do. Then the police, acting on your tip, get busy and solve the case by clever detective work. After we've solved the case you start trying to work your fix and we'll do everything we can up here. We'll tell you all we know and show you the ropes. If you can square it more power to you."

I nodded.

"But remember, Donald," he said, wagging a forefinger at me as though he'd been a schoolteacher and I was a naughty pupil, "don't try to slip anything over on us. If you know anything, you'd better tell us now. If you know something you aren't telling and we find it out, it's going to be too bad, just too bad."

"I understand."

"Not only for your client, but it's going to be too bad for your agency. We co-operate with people who co-operate with us, and we don't co-operate with people who don't co-operate with us."

"Suits me," I told him.

"Here's a list of the witnesses on that hit-and-run," he said, handing me a typewritten list of names and addresses. "That's all we have to work on at the moment. But I feel sure you're going to help us get more, Donald. I feel certain of it. You'll want it squared up, and you're not dumb.

"Now if there's anything you want while you're up here, any information we can get for you, don't hesitate for a minute. Just tell us what you want, Donald, and we'll get it for you." I thanked him and walked out.

I took a taxi to the Palace Hotel, paid off, ducked through to the side entrance, picked up another cab. A car was tailing me. I couldn't shake it off without tipping off the cab driver and making the driver of the car behind know I had him spotted.

I told the cabbie to drive along Bush Street. When I saw a rather pretentious apartment up near the top of the hill, I told the driver to stop and wait for me. I ran up the stairs, walked in to the desk, and handed the man on duty my card.

"I'm up here working on a case," I told him.

His eyes were exceedingly uncordial.

"Do you have a tenant," I asked, "who drives a very

dark blue Buick sedan?"

"I wouldn't know. It's quite possible we have several."

I frowned and said, "This is the address I have and it should be here, a dark-blue sedan."

"I'm sure I couldn't tell you."

"Could you find out for me?"

"I'm afraid not. We don't spy on our tenants."

"I don't want you to spy on anyone. I just want a little information. I *could* get a list of tenants and look up the registrations."

"Then why don't you do that, Mr. Lam?"

"Because I can save time this way."

"Time," he said, "is money."

I said, "In this case there isn't much money."

"Then you should have lots of time."

I said, "I'll see what I can do and come back."

"Do that."

I walked out, got in the taxicab, and went back to my hotel. I went up to my room, waited ten minutes, got in a cab, went out to Sutro Baths, and had myself a nice swim. When I got out of the baths I took a cab and started back along Geary Street. When I reached the cross street I wanted I paid off the cab and walked around the block. When I made sure no one was following me I stepped into a drugstore, called another cab, and went to the address of John Carver Billings. A maid answered my ring.

I said, "I'm Donald Lam from Los Angeles. I want to see John Carver Billings the Second, and you can tell him it's urgent and important."

"Just a moment," she said.

She looked at my card, then took the precaution of closing the door while she vanished inside the house. Two minutes later she was back and said, "Come in."

I went through a reception hall into a big drawing-room, and John Carver Billings the Second came forward to meet me. He was not at all pleased to see me.

"Why, hello, Lam! What the hell are you doing up here?"

"Working."

"I thought your agency did a very fine job for me," he said, "but that's all done—finished. *Pau*, as they say in Hawaii."

He didn't ask me to sit down.

I said, "I have another matter I'm working on."

"If there's anything in which I can assist you I'll be glad to do what I can." His voice was like cold linoleum on bare feet.

I said, "I'm investigating a hit-and-run case up here. The police are interested in it."

"You mean the police hired a private detective from Los Angeles to—"

"I didn't say that. I said the police were interested."

"In a hit-and-run case?"

"Yes."

"They should be."

"A fellow down on the corner of Post and Polk Streets," I said, "hit a man and broke him up a bit, then kept right on going. Someone tried to follow him and ran into a car that was just pulling out from the curb. That enabled the guy to make a getaway—temporarily."

"What are you trying to do? Find the fellow?"

"I think I know who he is," I said, looking him right in the eye. "I'm trying to find some way of fixing it up for him now."

"Well, I can't say I wish you any luck. These hit-and-run drivers are a menace. Was there anything else, Lam?"

I said, "Yes. Let's have a little talk."

"I'm rather busy now. I'm in conference with my father and—"

I said, "If you were sick and walked into a doctor's

office and asked him to give you a prescription for penicillin, he gave you one with no questions asked and let you walk out, what would you think?"

"I'd think he was a hell of a doctor. Is that what you want me to say?"

"That's what I want you to say."

"All right. I've said it."

I said, "That's what you did. You walked into a detective agency, described the medicine you wanted, and then walked out."

"I gave you a very specific assignment, if that's what you mean. There wasn't any medicine and I wasn't sick."

"You may not have *thought* you were sick but you'd better take another look at the situation. Try your pulse—and temperature."

"Just what are you driving at, Lam?"

I said, "You fixed up a fake alibi, then you went out and planted it. You wanted us to uncover it for you. In that way you could act very innocent and say that you'd paid good money to get a detective agency to find the people who—"

"I don't think I like your attitude, Lam."

"The weakness of such a scheme," I went on, "is that you don't dare to approach a perfect stranger. You have to get someone you're friendly with, and then your friendship for that person can be proven. Furthermore, in order to make Sylvia a fallen woman in name only, as well as to bolster your alibi, you insisted on having two people, so Sylvia got her friend Millie."

"Do you have any idea what you're talking about? Because I don't."

"And," I went on, "after you'd made certain we were going to handle the case and everything was all fixed, you went dashing out to that motor court, put on a leather jacket and gold-braided cap, and went in where you could plant the evidence for me to find.

"I don't know just how it happened that you picked that particular motor court. You may have stayed there before and thought there was a little something phony about it, or you may have just picked one at random.

"Now," I went on, "if I knew what you were trying to cover up on Tuesday night, I *might* be able to help you. That's what we're for. To help you if we can."

He said, very slowly, in cold anger, "I'd been warned about private detectives. I'd been told they tried to blackmail clients if they could get anything on those clients. I see now the warning was one that I should have heeded. I shall instruct my bank the first thing Monday morning to dishonor that check which was given to your agency. I am sending your agency a wire that payment on the check has been stopped. I don't appreciate your meddling in my private affairs; I don't appreciate your attempt at blackmail; and I don't like you."

I played the last card. "Your dad," I said, "might resent it if his son received a lot of publicity as being the driver of the hit-and-run car. There is always the chance that we can square these things and—"

"Just a minute," he said, "wait right there, Lam. I have something for you. That last remark really gave me an idea. Wait right there, don't go away."

He turned and left the room.

I walked over to a comfortable chair and sat down.

Steps sounded, a door opened, and Billings was back in the room with an older man.

"This is my father," he said. "I have no secrets from him. Dad, this is Donald Lam. He's a private detective from Los Angeles. I hired his firm to find out the people who were with me Tuesday night in a motor court in Los Angeles. He did an excellent job of getting the people located. I have his report here in writing showing that he located and talked with at least one of them, and that everything is exactly as I reported it to him.

"I gave his agency a check for a five-hundred-dollar bonus in accordance with an understanding I made with them. I am not at all certain it was ethical for me to do that. I think perhaps that constituted a contingency fee and may be a breach of ethics on the part of the agency.

"Now he shows up and tries to blackmail me. He accuses me of having tried to fake an alibi and *is* intimating that I was mixed up in a hit-and-run charge Tuesday night, some accident which I believe occurred near Post and Polk. What shall I do?"

John Carver Billings the First looked at me as though I might have been something that had just crawled under a crack in the door and he wanted to get a good look at me before he stepped on me.

"Throw the son of a bitch out," he said.

"Your son wasn't in that motor court Tuesday night. He's been trying to fix up a fake alibi. He's made a clumsy job of it and if there should be any investigation the very fact that he had tried to fix up that fake alibi would fasten the brand of guilt on him, and at the same time alienate the sympathy of the court and the public. I'm simply trying to help the guy."

The elder Billings continued to regard me with cold, patronizing scorn. "Are you quite finished, Mr.—Mr.—"

"Lam. Donald Lam."

"Are you quite finished, Mr. Lam?"

"Quite."

Billings turned to his son. "Just what's this all about, John?"

John moistened his lips with his tongue. "Dad, I'll tell you the truth. I was on the loose in L.A. I picked up a girl. All I did was ask her to dance. After that *she* picked *me* up. Then she stood me up.

"It turned out this girl was the moll of a notorious gangster. Now she's disappeared.

"After she stood me up I fell in with a couple of nice girls from here. I didn't know their names. The three of us spent the night in a motor court.

"I hired this man to find out who the girls were so I could, if necessary, prove that I wasn't with this moll, Maurine Auburn.

"He did a good job of finding them. Now he's trying to invalidate the result of his own investigation. He may have been given money or he may want some. Or it may be that one of the girls who hated my guts has lied to this man so she can cut herself a piece of cake."

"That's all you have to tell me, John?"

"So help me, Dad, that's all."

Billings turned to me. "There's the door. Get out."

I smiled at him. "Now," I said, "*you* interest me."

He walked over to the telephone, picked it up, and said, "Police headquarters, please."

I said, "Lieutenant Sheldon is the man you want to ask for. Sheldon is investigating a hit-and-run accident that took place on Post and Polk Streets Tuesday night at about ten-thirty."

John Carver Billings the First never turned a hair. He said into the telephone, "Yes. Is this police headquarters? . . . I want to speak with Lieutenant Sheldon."

It could have been a bluff. There might have been a switch that kept the phone from being connected. I couldn't tell.

I waited. A moment later the receiver made a squawking noise, and Billings said, "This is John Carver Billings, Lieutenant. I am being annoyed by a private detective who apparently is trying to blackmail my son. . . . He has given me your name. . . . What's that? Yes, a private detective from Los Angeles. The name is Donald Lam."

"The firm name is Cool and Lam, Dad," his son prompted.

"I believe he is of the firm of Cool and Lam of Los Angeles," the old man went on. "He apparently is trying to find a fall guy to take the place of some client who quite apparently was mixed up in a hit-and-run case last Tuesday night. . . . Yes, yes, that's it. That's what he said. At Polk and Post Streets at about ten-thirty. . . . That's the one. What shall I do? Shall I? . . . Very well, I'll try to hold him until you can get here."

I didn't wait to hear any more. If it was a bluff they had more blue chips than I did, and they sure as hell had pushed theirs into the center of the table, the whole damn stack. I turned around and walked out.

No one made any effort to stop me.

Chapter Eight

Two taxicabs later I found myself on the south side of Market. It wasn't a dive, it was a dump. It was good enough for what I wanted. It had to be.

At a little store on Third Street I picked up a shirt, some socks, and underwear. A drugstore sold me shaving things. Then in the dingy, stuffy inside room I sat down at a rickety little table and started checking over what had happened.

John Carver Billings the Second had needed an alibi and his need had been so urgent that he had spent a great deal of money, time, and effort in a clumsy attempt to fabricate something that would stand up.

Why?

The most logical thing was the hit-and-run charge, but that hadn't seemed to faze him when I put it up to him.

Therefore he was either a better poker player than I figured, or I was on the wrong track.

I went down to a phone booth and phoned Elsie Brand at her apartment. Luckily I found her in.

"How's Sylvia?" she asked.

"Sylvia's fine," I told her. "She wanted to be remembered to you."

"Thank her very much," she said icily.

"Elsie, I think I'm on the wrong trail up here."

"How come?"

"I don't know. It bothers me. I think perhaps the answer may have been in Los Angeles, after all. I wish you'd start pulling wires down there and get a list of all of the crimes that were committed in Los Angeles on Tuesday night."

"That's going to be quite a list."

"Specialize first on the hit-and-run charges," I said. "I'm looking for a case where a pedestrian was hit, badly injured, and the car wasn't hurt enough so there were any clues left on the spot. Do you get me?"

"I get you."

I said, "That also might cover anything in the immediate vicinity of Los Angeles. Oh, say, within fifty or a hundred miles. See what you can do, will you?"

"Is it urgent?"

"It's urgent."

She said, "You don't care a thing about a girl's weekend, do you?"

"You'll have lots of weekends after I get back," I told her.

"And a lot of good they'll do me," she retorted.

"What was that last?"

"I simply said to give my love to Sylvia," she observed, and then asked, "Where can I call you?"

"You can't. I'll call you."

"When?"

"Sometime tomorrow morning."

"Sunday morning!"

"That's right."

"You're getting more and more like Bertha every day," she told me.

"Okay," I said. "I'll give you more time and more sleep. Let's make it at the office Monday morning. I'll call collect because I'm running short of cash."

"Make it Sunday if you want, Donald. Anything I can do—"

"No, you won't be able to get the information by then."

"How do you know? A police detective is buying my dinner tonight."

"You *do* get around."

"Just local stuff. *I* don't need to go to another city."

I laughed. "Make it Monday, Elsie. That'll be soon enough."

"Honest?"

"Honest."

" 'By now," she said softly, and hung up.

I went out to Post and Polk and looked around. It was a nice intersection for an accident. Someone coming along Post Street and seeing a Go signal at Van Ness would start speeding to try and make the signal if he thought he had a clear run for it at Polk Street.

A kid was selling newspapers on the corner. There was quite a bit of traffic.

I took from my pocket the list of witnesses that Lieutenant Sheldon had given me and wondered if it was complete.

There was a woman whose occupation was listed simply as a saleslady, a man who worked in a nearby drugstore, a motorist who "saw it all" from a place midway in the block, and a man who ran a little cigar stand had heard the crash, and run out to see what it was all about.

There wasn't anything about a newsboy.

I started thinking that over, then I walked up and bought a paper, gave the kid two bits, and told him to keep the change.

"This your regular beat?" I asked.

He nodded, his sharp eyes studying the people and the traffic, looking for an opportunity to sell another paper.

"Here every night?"

He nodded.

I said suddenly, "How come you didn't tell the police what you knew about that hit-and-run case last Tuesday night?"

He would have started to run if I hadn't grabbed his arm. "Come on, kid," I said, "let's have it."

He looked like a trapped rabbit. "You can't come busting up and start pushing me around like this."

"Who's pushing you around?"

"You are."

"You haven't seen anything yet," I told him. "How much money did they pay you to clam up?"

"Go roll a hoop."

"That," I told him, "is what is known as compounding a felony."

"I've got some friends on the force here," he said. "Fellows that aren't going to stand for having me pushed around."

"You may have some friends on the force," I said, "but you're not dealing with the force now. Do you know any good judges?"

I saw him wince at that.

"Of course," I said, "a good friend who is a judge *might* help you. This isn't the police. I'm private, and I'm tough."

"Aw, what are you picking on me for? Give a guy a break, can't you?"

"What difference does it make to you?" I asked him.

"Did somebody give you money?"

"Of course not."

"Perhaps trying a little blackmail?"

"Aw, have a heart, mister. Gee, I was going to play it on the square and then I realized I couldn't."

"Why couldn't you?"

"Because I was in trouble down in Los Angeles. I skipped parole. I ain't supposed to be selling papers. I'm supposed to be reporting to a probation officer every thirty days and all that stuff. I didn't like it and I came up here and been going straight."

"Why didn't you report the hit-and-run?"

"How could I? I thought I was going to be smart. I took down the guy's number and figured I'd make a grandstand with the cops, and then I suddenly realized what it would mean. The D.A. would call me as a witness and the smart guy who was defending the fellow would start ripping me up the back and down the front and show that I had skipped out on parole, the jury wouldn't believe me, and I'd get sent back to L.A. as a parole violator."

"Pretty smart for a kid, aren't you?"

"I ain't a kid."

I looked down into the prematurely wise little face with the sharp eyes sizing me up, studying me for a weak point where he could take advantage of me, felt the bony little shoulder under my hand, and said, "Okay, kid. You play square with me and I'll play square with you. How old are you?"

"Seventeen."

"How are you getting along up here?"

"I'm doing good. I'm keeping on the straight and narrow. The trouble down in L.A. I had too many friends. I'd get out with the gang and they'd start calling me sissy if I didn't ride along."

"What were they doing?"

"Believe me, mister, they were getting so they were doing damn near everything. It started out with kid stuff, then when Butch got to be head of the outfit he said the only fellows who could run with the gang were the ones who had guts enough to be regular guys. I mean he's tough."

"Why didn't you go to the probation officer and tell him all that?"

"Think I was going to rat?"

"Why didn't you just stay home and mind your own business?"

"Don't be silly."

"So you took a powder and came up here?"

"That's right."

"And you're going straight?"

"Like a string."

"Give me the license number and I'll try to keep you out of it."

He pulled a scrap of paper from his pocket that had been torn from the edge of a newspaper. On it was scribbled a number, written with a hard pencil so that it was all but illegible.

I studied it carefully.

He went on in an eager, whining voice. "That's the car that hit the guy. The driver came tearing down the hill and almost hit me. That's when I got so mad I started to take his number. He was a fat, middle-aged guy with a little blonde plastered up against him. She started to kiss him just as they got to the corner, or he was kissing her, or they were kissing each other, I don't know which."

"What did you do?"

"I jumped out of the way and thought the guy was going to crash into the curb. I took his number—that is, I got out the pencil and was writing it down on the edge of the paper when he smacked right into this guy."

"Then what?"

"Then he slowed down for a minute and I thought he was stopping; then the wren said something to him and changed his mind. He stepped on it."

"No one after him?"

"Sure. A guy tried to nail him just as some goof swung out from the curb. They smashed up and littered the street with broken glass. By that time people were running around giving help to the old man, and all of a sudden I realized that I was in a spot; that if I told the police who the fellow was I'd be a gone coon."

"Who was he?"

"I tell you I don't know. All I know is he was driving a dark sedan, he was going like hell, and he and this babe were pitching woo right up to the time they hit the street intersection."

"Drunk?"

"How do I know? He was busy doing other things besides driving the automobile. Now I've given you a break, mister. Let me go."

I handed him five dollars. "Go buy yourself a Coca-Cola, buddy, and quit worrying about it."

He looked at the five for a moment, then swiftly crumpled it and shoved it down into his pocket. "That all?" he asked.

I said, "Would you know this gent if you saw him again, the one who was driving the car?"

He looked at me with eyes that were suddenly hard and shrewd. "No," he said.

"Couldn't recognize him if you saw him in a line-up?"

"No."

I left the newsboy and looked up the registration of the number he had given me.

It was Harvey B. Ludlow and he lived in an apartment way out on the beach. The car was a Cadillac sedan.

Chapter Nine

I slept until noon Sunday, in my south-of-Market dump. Breakfast at a nearby restaurant consisted of stale eggs fried in near-rancid grease, muddy coffee, and cold, soggy toast.

I got the Sunday papers, and went back to my stuffy room with its threadbare carpet, hard chair, and stale stench.

Gabby Garvanza had made news of a sort.

He'd discharged himself from the hospital, and his departure had given every indication that he was a worried, apprehensive man.

He had, in fact, simply vanished into thin air.

His nurses and physician insisted they knew nothing about it.

Garvanza was recuperating nicely and had been able to travel under his own power. Attired in pajamas, slippers, and bathrobe, he had announced his intention of walking down the hall to the solarium.

When his special nurse went to the solarium a few minutes later she drew a blank. A frantic search of the hospital yielded no clues and no Gabby Garvanza.

Theories ranged from the fact that the gambler had taken a run-out powder to abduction by the enemies who had tried to rub him out.

The mobster had left behind clothes which had been taken to him by Maurine Auburn on the day following the shooting.

The three-hundred-and-fifty-dollar suit of clothes, the silk shirt, and the twenty-five-dollar hand-painted tie which he had been wearing on the night he was shot, had been impounded as evidence. The bullet holes in the bloodstained garments were expected to yield perhaps some clue on spectrographic analysis as to the composition of the slugs which had penetrated Garvanza's body.

The day after the shooting Maurine Auburn had brought a suitcase containing another three-hundred-and-fifty-dollar tailor-made suit, a pair of seventy-five-dollar made-to-order shoes, another twenty-five-dollar hand-painted necktie, and an assortment of silk shirts, socks, and handkerchiefs.

All of these had been left behind. When he vanished the gambler had been wearing only bathrobe, pajamas, and slippers.

The hospital staff insisted that a man so clothed could not possibly leave the hospital by any of the exits, and pointed out that it would be virtually impossible for him to get a cab while clad in that attire.

Police retorted that whether or not it had been possible, Gabby had disappeared, and that he hadn't needed a cab.

There was some criticism of the police for not posting a guard, but the police countered that criticism with the fact that Gabby Garvanza had been the target. He had not done any shooting and had, in fact, been unarmed at the time he was shot. Police had other and more important duties than to assign a bodyguard for a notorious gambler who seemed to be having troubles with competition that wished to muscle in on what the press referred to as "a lucrative racket"—despite the fact that the police insisted the town was closed up tight and there was no gambling worthy of the name.

I took my knife, cut the clipping out of the newspaper, and folded it in my wallet.

Since I was, for the moment, at a standstill, and since I dared not circulate around too freely, I spent a long, tiresome day reading, thinking, and keeping under cover.

Monday I went out to get a morning paper.

The story was on the front page.

The body of Maurine Auburn had been found buried in a shallow grave near Laguna Beach, the famous ocean and resort city south of Los Angeles.

A shallow grave had been dug in the sand above high-tide line, but air had seeped through the loose sand, the odor of decomposition had become noticeable, and the body had been uncovered.

From its location authorities felt the grave had been hastily dug at night, and that the young woman was already dead when a car drove down a side street, stopped near a cliff, and the body was dumped over the cliff to the sand below. The murderer then had hastily scooped out a grave in the soft sand and made his escape.

From an examination of the body, the coroner believed she had been dead about a week. She had been shot twice in the back—a cold-blooded, efficient job. Either bullet would have resulted in almost instant death.

Both of the fatal bullets had been recovered.

Los Angeles police, who had been inclined to wash their hands of the attractive moll after her distinct refusal to co-operate in giving the police information concerning the shooting of Gabby Garvanza, now had no comment to make. The sheriff of Orange County was breathing smoke, fire, and threats to gangsters.

In view of these developments, search was being redoubled for a young man with whom it was known Maurine Auburn had disappeared on the night that police now felt certain was the night of her death. Police had a good description and were making a "careful check."

I went to a phone booth and rang up Elsie Brand at the office, putting through the call collect.

I heard the operator at the other end of the line say, "Mrs. Cool said she would take any collect calls from Donald Lam."

A moment later I heard Bertha's hysterical voice screaming oven the wire. "You damn little moron. What do you think *you're* doing? Who the hell do you think is masterminding this business?"

"What's the matter now?" I asked.

"What's the matter?" she yelled. "We're in a jam. You've tried to blackmail a client. They're going to revoke our license. The client has stopped payment on the five-hundred-dollar bonus check. What's the matter? What's the matter? You go sticking your neck out there in San Francisco. The San Francisco police have a pickup on you, the agency is in bad, the five hundred dollars has gone down the drain, and you're calling collect. What the hell do you think's the matter?"

"I want to get some information from Elsie Brand," I said.

"Pay for the call, then," Bertha screamed. "There won't be any more collect calls on the phone at this end."

She slammed up the receiver so that it must have all but pulled the phone out by the roots.

I hung up the telephone, sat there in the booth, and counted my available cash.

I didn't have enough to squander any money on telephoning Elsie Brand.

I went to the telegraph office and sent her a collect telegram.

WIRE ME INFORMATION PREPAID WILL CALL WESTERN UNION BRANCH FIRST AND MARKET.

Bertha probably wouldn't think to stop collect telegrams.

I went back to my hole-in-the-wall hotel and kicked my heels, marking time while waiting for information.

The noon editions of the San Francisco newspapers blossomed out with useful information. The killing of Maurine Auburn suddenly assumed importance because it had a swell local angle.

Headlines across the front page said: *Son of Wealthy Banker Volunteers Information in Gangster Killing.*

I read that John Carver Billings the Second had voluntarily reported to police that he had been the one who had asked Maurine Auburn to dance at an afternoon rendezvous spot, that he had been the one whose fascination had charmed the attractive "moll" into leaving her companions.

The young man's amatory triumph, however, had been swiftly eclipsed by humiliation when the moll had gone to "powder her nose" and had failed to reappear.

Young Billings reported that he had thereafter "become acquainted" with two San Francisco girls, and had spent the "rest of the evening" with them. He had not known their names until he had located them through the efforts of a Los Angeles detective agency which had uncovered the identity of the two young women.

Billings had given police the names of these two women, and, since they were reputable young ladies employed in San Francisco business establishments, and inasmuch as it seemed their contact with Billings had consisted merely in making a round of night spots and using him to "show them the town," police were withholding their names. It was known, however, that they had been interviewed and had confirmed Billings's story in every detail.

The newspaper carried an excellent picture of John Carver Billings, a good, clear photograph taken by a newspaper photographer.

I went around to the newspaper office and hunted up the art department. A couple of two-bit cigars got me a fine glossy print of the picture, a real likeness of John Carver Billings the Second.

I strolled back to the telegraph office. There was no wire from Elsie.

I took a streetcar to Millie Rhodes's apartment.

I found her home.

"Oh, hello," she said. "Come on in."

Her eyes were sparkling with excitement. She was wearing an outfit which evidently had just been removed from a box bearing the label of one of San Francisco's most expensive stores.

"No work?" I asked.

"Not today," she said, smiling enigmatically.

"I thought your vacation was up and you were due back to work."

"I changed my plans."

"And the job?"

"I'm a lady of leisure."

"Since when?"

"That's telling."

"Like it?"

"Don't be silly."

"You're burning bridges, Millie."

"Let 'em burn."

"You might want to go back."

"Not me. I'm going places, not going back—ever."

"That's a new suit, isn't it?"

"Isn't it divine? It does things for me. I found it and it fits me as though it had been made for me. It didn't need the slightest alteration. I'm crazy about it."

She had been standing in front of the full-length mirror. Now she raised her hands slightly and turned slowly around so I could see the lines.

"It's a nice job," I said. "It does things for you."

She sat down, crossed her legs, and smoothed the skirt over her knees with a caressing motion.

"Well," she said, "what is it this time?"

I said, "I don't want you burning bridges. It was all right to lie to me about the John Carver Billings alibi."

"John Carver Billings *the Second*," she amended with a smile.

"The Second," I admitted. "Lying to me was one thing—lying to the police is another."

"Look, Donald," she said, "you look like a nice boy. You're a detective. That makes you have a nasty, suspicious mind. You came here and intimated that I was lying in order to give John Carver Billings the Second an alibi. I rode along with you in order to see what you'd say."

I said, "You broke down on cross-examination, and couldn't tell a consistent story."

She laughed as though the whole thing was very amusing. "I was just sounding you out, Donald, riding along with the gag."

She moved over to the davenport and sat down beside me, put one hand on my shoulder, said softly, "Donald, why don't you grow up?"

"I've grown up."

"You can't buck money and influence—not in this town."

"Who has the money?" I asked angrily.

"Right at the moment," she said, "John Carver Billings the Second has money."

"All right. Who has the influence?"

"I'll answer that question. John Carver Billings."

"You left off *the Second*," I told her sarcastically.

"No, I didn't."

"You mean that?"

She nodded. "I mean John Carver Billings, the old man. He's calling the turns."

I thought that over.

She said, "You stuck your neck out. You did things you shouldn't have done. You said things you shouldn't have said. Why didn't you ride along, Donald?"

"Because I'm not built that way."

"You've lost five hundred dollars, you've got yourself in bad with the police, there's an order out to pick you up, and you're in a sweet mess. Now, *if* you wanted to grow up and be your age you could have that all straightened out. The police would withdraw their pickup order, the five-hundred-dollar check would be reinstated, and everything would be hunky-dory."

"So you've gone back to the alibi story."

"I never abandoned the alibi story."

"You did to me."

"That's what *you* say."

"You know you did."

She said almost dreamily, "John Carver Billings the Second, Sylvia Tucker, and I all tell the same story. You come along and *claim* that I changed my story to you. I deny it. John Carver Billings the Second says you tried to blackmail him. Police say you were snooping around trying to get something which you could use to blackmail a client. *That's* not being smart, Donald."

"So you've decided to sell me out?"

"No. I've decided to buy me in."

"You can't get away with it, Millie. Don't try it," I pleaded.

"You run your business. I'll run mine."

"Millie, you can't do it. You can't get away with it. Within two minutes of the time I started to cross-examine you, you had yourself all mixed up."

"Try cross-examining me now."

"What good would it do if I trapped you again? You'd simply be that much wiser and you'd lie out of it."

"I'm wise now, Donald. Why don't *you* get wise?"

I said, "You're dealing with a bunch of amateurs. They think they can fix things up. You're a nice girl, Millie. I hate to see you get mixed up in this thing. You could get in pretty bad over this."

"You're the one who's in bad now."

I started for the door and said angrily, "Stick around and see who's in bad."

She came running to me. "Don't leave like that, Donald."

I pushed her to one side.

Her arms were around me. "Look, Donald, you're a swell guy. I hate to see you get in bad. You're bucking power and influence and money. They'll crush you flat and throw you to one side. You'll be discredited, convicted of extortion, you'll lose your license. Donald, *please*. I can fix it all up for you. I told them they'd have to square things for you or I wouldn't go along. They promised."

I said, "Millie, let's look at it from the standpoint of cold-blooded logic. It cost John Carver Billings the Second almost a thousand dollars to manufacture that alibi, and that isn't taking into consideration what they paid you. I have an idea Sylvia was softhearted and they didn't pay her much. They paid you two hundred and fifty dollars the first time. When they came back this second time they *really* decorated the mahogany.

"You started buying clothes and suitcases. You're going to make an affidavit and then you're going traveling, perhaps a trip to Europe."

"All right," she said hotly, "they sent for me. They paid me money, *big* money, and they gave me the protection of influence, *big* influence. I'm not going to Europe. I'm going to South America. Do you know what that means?"

"Sure I know what it means," I said. "You're making an affidavit and then you're getting on a boat, where, for a time at least, you'll be out of the jurisdiction of the court. They can only question you by interrogations forwarded through the American Consulate. You'll—"

"It isn't that," she said. "You're looking at it from the other person's viewpoint. I am looking at it from my viewpoint.

"Do you know what it means when a girl comes to the city and gets on her own? She doesn't have any difficulty meeting a lot of boys—playboys. That's all they want to do, play.

"At the start you think you'd like a little playing yourself. You're on the loose. For the first time in your life you're grown up, with all that it means. You're an individual, completely free and unhampered. You have an apartment, you are your own boss, you're making your own living. You don't have to ask anybody for anything. Or, that's what you think. You feel there's lots of time to settle down whenever you get ready. You have a job and you're getting a regular paycheck. You can buy clothes and you can do what you want when you want.

"It's a fine sensation for a while and then the sugar coating wears off and you begin to taste the bitter that's underneath.

"You're not independent. You're a cog in the economic and social machine. You can get just so high and no higher. If you want to play you can get acquainted with a lot of playboys. If you want anything else you're stymied.

"After a while you begin to think about security. You begin to think about a home, about children, about—about being respectable. You want to have some one man whom you can love and respect, to whom you can devote your life. You want to have kids and watch them grow up. You want to have a husband and a home.

"You don't meet anybody who wants to be a husband or to make a home. You're tagged as a playgirl. You've been having fun and there's a tag on you. The homely little bookkeeper marries the bashful guy in the filing-department. You don't get proposals. You get propositions. The headwaiters all know you and make a fuss over you— You're tagged.

"The married men at the office all make passes at you

in their spare time. The boss slaps your fanny, tells you an off-color joke or two, and thinks he's being devilish. You meet a lot of guys who look all right on the surface and who swear they're bachelors on the loose. After the fifth drink they pull a wallet out of their pocket and show you pictures of the wife and kids."

"I'm going on a boat, Donald. No one's going to know anything about me or about my background. I'll have good clothes. I'll be chic and interesting. I'll sit in a deck chair and have all day to look over the passengers. I'll spot the ones who are eligible."

"And throw your hooks into the first one you can get?" I asked.

"I'm not that anxious," she said, "and I'm not that low, but if I find someone who interests me and find that I'm interesting him, I'll have an opportunity to talk with him, to find out what kind of a chap he is, what he wants out of life. I'll really get acquainted.

"The way it is now, somebody introduces me to a good-looking fellow. He wants to take me to dinner. I rush home and take a shower, put on a party dress and war paint. We go out to dinner. He shows what he wants and what he expects inside of the first ten minutes. From then on it's the same old routine and it turns out he's a buyer from Los Angeles who has a wife and two kids. He's crazy about his family but he thinks he's a wolf, and I'm supposed to ride along.

"I'd like to spend an *afternoon* with a man sometime. I'd like to visit and get acquainted with new people. I'd like to go ashore in Rio de Janeiro and prowl through the shops with some interesting man who wasn't thinking in terms of making your acquaintance, getting a pass to first base, stealing second, and crossing the home plate, all within two hours."

I said, "You've been reading the steamship ads; somebody's handed you a bunch of folders with pictures of a girl and a fellow outlined against a path of moonlight in tropical waters, with pictures of happy couples dancing to the rhythm of romantic music. You—"

"Don't, Donald," she said, laughing. "You're taking all the joy out of it."

There was a catch in her laugh. I turned to look at her. Her eyes were filled with tears.

I said, "You came here, Millie. You got in with a carefree bunch. Your friends are that type. All right, so you're tagged. But why not go to a new place, get a job, make new friends?"

"How you talk!" she interrupted. "I'd have to give up everything I've worked for. I'd start out on a starvation salary and I'd die of loneliness.

"I need action, Donald. I want to get out and circulate. I want to see people. I crave action and variety. I'm no stick-in-the-mud. I'm no stay-at-home. I want to see good shows, listen to good music, dance at the best night spots. I want luxury."

"You can't have all that unless you have the connections—or money."

"I can if I travel first-class."

I said, "It's a swell air castle, Millie, but you can't get away with it."

"Don't tell me I can't get away with it."

"You'll wind up facing a charge of perjury."

"Don't throw cold water, Donald. I've made a date with fortune. I'm going to keep it. Lots of times in my life I've been tempted not to do the things I wanted to do because of things that conceivably could happen. I've always found out that lots of things happened, but none of the things I was afraid would happen. If you don't do something you want to do you very definitely haven't done it. That's final and complete and you'll probably regret it. If you do what you want to do, you may get into a mess, but getting into the mess and getting out of the mess is better than shutting yourself up in a closet and hiding from life. Donald, I'm going through with it. I'm leaving for Rio."

"When?" I asked.

She smiled. "The when and the how are secrets I'm not supposed to discuss, but I'm going and you'd be surprised if you knew how soon."

"Okay," I told her. "It's your funeral."

"Wrong," she said. "It's my wedding."

"Send me an invitation, will you?"

"I sure will, Donald—Donald?"

"What?"

"Are *you* married?"

There was a wistful half-smile on her lips.

"No," I said, and opened the door.

"I knew that would do it," she said as I stepped out into the corridor.

I went to the Western Union Office and sent Elsie Brand another wire collect.

DISREGARD ALL CRIMES EXCEPT MURDER. STAKES ARE TOO BIG FOR ANYTHING SMALLER WIRE REPLY RUSH.

Chapter Ten

I had a bowl of chili and went to the telegraph office.

A wire was waiting for me.

NO MURDERS ACTUALLY COMMITTED BUT ONE THREATENED IN THE OFFICE. YOU HAVE OF COURSE READ ABOUT MAURINE. COULD THIS BE THE ANSWER OR IS THAT TOO SIMPLE? LOVE.
                                            ELSIE.

I was putting the message in my pocket when the operator said, "Wait a minute, Mr. Lam, here's another one coming in for you. It's longer."

I sat around and waited while one of the operators took tape from a Teletype and pasted it on a message.

When they finally handed it to me I saw the clerk looking at me with that type of curiosity the average public reserves for famous criminals, private detectives, and prostitutes.

"Sign here," she said.

I signed.

The message read:

FOR YOUR INFORMATION G.G. WHO TOOK POWDER FROM HOSPITAL IS ABOARD UNITED AIRLINES FLIGHT NUMBER 665 LEAVING LOS ANGELES THREE P.M. ARRIVING SAN FRANCISCO AIRPORT FOUR-THIRTY TODAY. HE IS TRAVELING UNDER NAME GEORGE GRANBY AND THINKS HE IS ALL COVERED UP. I GOT IT FROM CONNECTION MENTIONED ON PHONE SO KEEP CONFIDENTIAL. BERTHA BLOWING TOP EVERY THIRTY MINUTES LIKE OLD FAITHFUL GEYSER IN YELLOWSTONE. YOU MUST BE LOW ON MONEY UNABLE CHISEL FROM FIRM BUT AM SENDING YOU LOAN FROM PRIVATE SAVINGS TRY TO MAKE IT LAST AS THERE ISN'T ANY MORE. ALL MY LOVE TO SYLVIA. YOURS.

It was signed, *Elsie*.

"Do you," asked the person behind the counter, "have anything to show your identity? A business card, a driving license, things of that sort?"

I showed her my driving license and my business card as a private investigator.

"Sign here," she said.

I signed.

She started counting out money. Three hundred and fifty dollars in twenties and tens. It was one of the most welcome sights I had ever seen.

Gabby Garvanza's plane would already be in, but I made a list of five of the principal hotels and started calling, asking if they had a George Granby registered.

In the third hotel I struck pay dirt. George Granby was registered and was in.

I waited on the line until a voice that sounded sullen and a little resentful said, "Hello."

I said, "I want to talk to you about the Maurine Auburn case. I'm a private detective from Los Angeles. I've been cutting corners and the police have issued a pickup on me. I don't want to be picked up and I don't want to be quoted. I want to talk."

Gabby Garvanza lived up to his reputation of being taciturn.

"Come up," he said, and slipped the phone back on the receiver.

I took a taxi to the hotel and went up to George Granby's room without being announced.

"Come in," a voice called as I knocked on the door.

I hesitated.

"Come on in, the door's unlocked."

I opened the door.

The room seemed empty.

I stepped inside and could see no one.

Abruptly the door was kicked shut. The heavy-set gorilla who had been standing behind the door came toward me.

The bathroom door opened and a sallow-looking man, who was evidently Gabby Garvanza, closed in from the other side.

"Up," the heavy-set man said.

I elevated my hands.

He was a big, burly fellow with a cauliflower ear and a face which showed the ravages of conflict. He gave me a complete and thorough frisking.

"He's clean," he said.

Gabby Garvanza said, "Sit down. Tell me who you are and what the hell you want."

I sat down and said, "I'm interested in finding out what happened to Maurine Auburn."

"Who isn't?"

I said, "I'm a private detective. I'm working on a case."

I handed him a card.

He barely glanced at the card, tossed it to one side, then thought better of it, took it up, looked at it again, gave it thoughtful consideration, and pushed it in his pocket.

"You've got a nerve, Lam."

I said nothing.

"How did you find me?"

"I'm a detective."

"That doesn't tell me anything."

"Think it over and it will."

"I don't like to think. You do it—out loud."

I shook my head.

"I'm supposed to be under cover," Gabby went on. "If it's that easy to lift the cover I want to know about it."

I said, "I'm here. Therefore it's that easy."

"How?"

"I don't know. I only know I have connections. They know I'm protecting them."

He said, "You talk big as hell for a little guy."

"That makes for a fair average," I told him.

He laughed at that and said, "I like your guts."

"Thanks."

"What's your problem?" Gabby asked after a minute.

I said, "It involves John Carver Billings the Second, the fellow who said he was with Maurine when she walked out on the party she was with."

"Go on."

"That's all."

He shook his head.

I said, "I'm interested in finding out where John Carver Billings was that night."

"What's stopping you?"

"Nothing."

"Go ahead and find out, then."

"That's what I'm doing."

"You're not getting very far here."

I grinned and lit a cigarette.

The bodyguard looked at Gabby, questioning him with a glance whether I should be tossed out of the window or kicked out into the corridor.

I blew out the match and said, "Young Billings *says* he picked up Maurine and then went out to a nitery and she went into the powder room and never came out."

"Sound reasonable to you?" he asked.

"No," I said.

"Keep talking," he invited.

I said, "The way I size it up, Maurine Auburn was out with fellows that know their way around. They were giving her protection. Young Billings tells a nice story about drifting in and picking her up and taking her away from the party she was with, just as though she'd been some secretary out with a couple of filing clerks and accountants from the office. I don't think it would have happened that way."

"Keep on thinking—out loud."

"So," I said, "I hate to see young Billings getting in bad over something he didn't do, something he couldn't have done. And I wondered if perhaps you came up here to question him."

Gabby Garvanza laughed.

I quit talking.

"Go on," Garvanza said.

"That's all there is."

"There's the door."

I shook my head and said, "I want to know whether you're going to question young Billings, whether you're going to check up on him, whether that's why you came up here, whether—"

"Go peddle your papers," the bodyguard said.

I sat still.

Gabby Garvanza nodded his head. The bodyguard came toward me.

I said, "I might be in a position to do you a favor sometime."

"Hold it," Gabby said to the bodyguard.

"Not now," I told him. "Later."

"How much later?"

"When I find out why a man should jump into the frying pan."

"Well, why did he?"

"There's only one possible reason—to get out of the fire."

"What fire?"

"That's what I'm looking for."

"When and if you find it, you could get the hell burned out of your fingers."

"They've been burned before. I'm wearing gloves."

"I don't see 'em."

"I had to take them off to come here."

"I'll say you did."

Gabby Garvanza thought things over, then said, "You haven't any idea how uninterested I am in this Billings guy."

"His story indicates you should be interested."

"His story stinks."

"You don't believe it?"

Gabby said, "You're a credulous guy. A Hollywood sport in plus fours comes in and tells you about how he walked into a lion's den, grabbed a chunk of horse meat away from a lion, slapped his face, and walked out, and so you go to ask the lion if it's true."

"Are you the lion?"

Gabby met my eyes and said, "You ask too many questions, but your nerve interests me. I've told you all I'm telling. Now get the hell out of here."

The bodyguard jerked the door open.

I went out.

Going down in the elevator I did a lot of thinking. John Carver Billings the Second must have picked a murder case that he thought he could beat because he was afraid that otherwise he might get mixed up in a murder case he couldn't beat.

There wasn't any murder recorded in San Francisco on that date, but I felt certain I'd been overlooking a bet. I decided to check the list of missing persons. There was just a chance I might find someone who had disappeared on Tuesday night.

I called our San Francisco correspondent, told him I was under cover, to check the list of missing persons, with special reference to Tuesday night, and bill the Los Angeles office. I told him I'd call later for the information.

Chapter Eleven

The evening newspapers saved me the trouble of asking my correspondent for a report. I read those papers and had the answer—or thought I did. It was the only answer I could find.

One George Bishop, a wealthy mining man, had left San Francisco Tuesday night to go to his mine in northern California.

He had never arrived.

Early today, the papers reported, his Cadillac automobile had been found where it had been driven off the road above Petaluma. There were blood spatters on the left-hand side of the front seat, and definite blood spatters on the *inside* of the windshield.

From the indications on the ground officers decided the automobile had been there for at least five days, perhaps longer. Putting two and two together, it looked as though Bishop had been waylaid late Tuesday night, probably by hitchhikers whom he had picked up and who had killed and robbed their benefactor.

It was known Bishop was in the habit of carrying large sums of cash with him on his business trips. On this trip he had expected to drive nearly all night in order to reach his mine in Siskiyou County early Wednesday morning.

In the trunk of the car police found a suitcase and leather handbag, both of the most expensive design, and filled with George Bishop's personal wearing-apparel and toilet articles. Bishop's wife had made a positive identification.

Police were now making an intensive search for Bishop's body in the vicinity of the automobile. Judging from the position of the bloodstains it was assumed he had been killed by bullets fired by someone sitting in the back seat of his car. This led police to believe Bishop had picked up more than one hitchhiker. They reasoned that a lone hitchhiker would have been sitting in the front seat beside Bishop. If there had been two or three, however, the back seat would have been occupied.

From the nature of the blood spatters police were not at all certain two people had not been killed. At least one of the homicide experts felt that someone seated on the driver's right had either been killed or seriously wounded.

Police, trying to reconstruct Bishop's trip, felt that the car might have been driven some little distance after Bishop's body had been dumped out inasmuch as there was no sign of the body anywhere near the car.

The most intensive search was along the main traveled highway, the assumption being that the murderers would have disposed of the body as soon as possible, and only after that had been done would they have driven the automobile up the little-used side road and then down the narrow lane to the place where it had been found. The murderers hardly dared risk driving any great distance with the body in the car, according to police reasoning.

The paper published a photograph of Bishop's wife making an identification of the contents of the suitcase. The picture showed that she was a good-looking babe, and while she was supposed to have been "overcome with grief" she had, nevertheless, been carefully conscious of the camera angles at the time the picture was taken, or else the photographer had been pretty clever about posing her.

The address was out in Berkeley and I decided to have a look for myself.

Bertha would have approved of my economy. I was trying to keep Elsie Brand's money as intact as possible. I went by bus.

The bus let me off within three blocks of the place and when I got to it I found there were two official-looking automobiles parked in front of it. I waited for nearly half an hour, prowling around the neighborhood.

The place was quite some mansion, a half-hillside sweep of grounds with a big house, a view, a swimming-pool, and a back lot where tons of crushed rock had been dumped into a fill.

I felt there was a good big seventy-five thousand dollars

in real estate and improvements, and a lot more money was going to be spent on the place.

At the end of about a half hour the last car was driven away and when it was out of sight around the terraced turn in the road, I went boldly up the front steps and rang the bell.

A colored maid answered the door.

I didn't waste any time. I flipped a careless hand toward the left lapel of my coat, said, "Tell Mrs. Bishop I want to see her," and pushed on in without taking my hat off.

The maid said, "She's pretty tired now."

"So am I," I said, and, still with my hat on, walked over to slide one hip over a mahogany library table.

I felt certain no one was ever going to say anything to me about impersonating an officer. I could well imagine the chagrin of the police department if the maid got on the stand and said, "Yes, *sir!* I knew he was an officer from the way he acted. He didn't tell me nothin'. He just walked in with his hat on, so I knew he must be an officer."

The woman who entered the room after about three minutes was tired to the point of being mentally numb.

She wore a simple, dark-colored dress that had a V in front low enough to emphasize the creamy smoothness of her skin. She was brunette, slate-eyed, nice-figured, in the mid-twenties, and ready to drop in her tracks.

"What is it?" she said, without even bothering to look at me.

"I want to check up on some of your husband's associates."

"That's been done already a dozen times."

"Did he know anyone by the name of Meredith?" I asked.

"I don't know. I haven't heard him speak of any— Man or woman?"

"Man."

"I haven't heard him speak of any Meredith."

"Billings?" I asked.

For a swift instant I felt there was a startled flicker of expression in her eyes, then she said in the same flat, weary voice, "Billings— That name is familiar. I may have heard George use it."

"Can you tell me a little something about his trip?"

"But we've gone over this, over and over and over."

"Not with me, you haven't."

"Well, what's *your* interest in it?"

I said, "I'm trying to solve the case. I'm going to save you a little trouble."

"We don't know there is any case yet," she said. "They haven't found—found anything to justify their conclusions. George may be working on some sort of a secret deal and he might go to almost any lengths to conceal what he was doing."

I waited for her to look up from the carpet; then I said, "Do you seriously believe that, Mrs. Bishop?"

"No," she said.

Her eyes started to lower, then she raised them to mine once more. "Go on," she said, and this time I could see that her brain was coming out of the mental fog of weariness in which it had been wrapped.

"He has a mine up north?"

"Siskiyou County."

"A paying mine?"

"I don't know much about his business affairs."

"And he left Tuesday?"

"That's right. Along about seven o'clock in the evening."

"Wasn't that rather late?"

"He planned to drive most of the night."

"Did he make a habit of picking up hitchhikers?"

She said, "You keep going over and over the same

things. Who *are* you, anyway?"

"The name," I told her, "is Lam," and threw another question at her quick before she had a chance to think that over. "Just what did he say to you prior to his departure?"

She didn't fall for it. Her eyes kept fastened on me. "Just what's your capacity, Mr. Lam?" she asked.

"Sometimes a quart. The results are usually disastrous. I take it your husband was away a good deal of the time?"

"I mean what's your capacity with the police force?"

"Zero-zero-point-zero. If you'll answer my questions, Mrs. Bishop, instead of asking questions, we'll get finished a lot faster."

"If you'll answer my questions instead of throwing more questions at me, we may terminate the interview a lot faster," she said, angry now and very much alert. "Just who are you?"

I saw then she was going after it until she had an answer. I didn't want to appear to dodge around the bushes. I said, "I'm Donald Lam. I'm a private detective from Los Angeles. I'm working on a case that I think may have some angles to it that will be of some assistance."

"Assistance to whom?"

"To me."

"I thought so."

"And," I said, "perhaps to *you*."

"In what way?"

I said, "Just because you're beautiful is no sign you're dumb."

"Thank you. But you can skip all that stuff."

I said, "Your husband was wealthy."

"What if he was?"

"The newspaper gave his age as fifty-six."

"That's right."

"You're evidently a second wife."

"I'll put up with just about so much of this," she said,

"and then I'll have you thrown out."

"There was probably insurance," I went on. "If you're dumb enough to think that the police haven't suspected you of having a young lover, and planning to get rid of your stodgy, middle-aged husband so you could inherit his money and go places with the boy you really like, you're ivory from the ears up."

"I suppose, Mr. Lam, that the ultimate purpose of all this is to frighten me into retaining you at a handsome salary?"

"Wrong again."

"What is the purpose?"

"I'm working on another case. I think the solution to it may have a great deal to do with your husband and what may have happened to him. Are you interested?"

She said, "No," but didn't make any move to leave the room.

I said, "If you're guilty of anything at all, don't stick around and answer my questions. There's a phone over there. If you have anything on your conscience go call a good lawyer, tell your story to him and to no one else."

"And if I'm not guilty of anything?"

"If you're not guilty of anything at all, if there's nothing you're afraid to have the police find out, talk with me and I may be able to help you."

"If I'm not guilty of anything I don't need any help."

"That shows what an optimist *you* are. Sometime when you haven't anything else to do, get Professor Borchard's book *Convicting the Innocent*, and read the sixty-five cases of authenticated wrongful convictions that are set forth in that book. And, believe me, that's just scratching the surface."

"I don't have time to read."

"You will."

"What do you mean by that?"

I said, "Unless you show a little savvy you may be spending the long afternoon hours in a cell."

"That's a cheap, shoddy attempt to frighten me."

"It is," I admitted.

"Why are you doing it if you don't want money?"

"I want information."

"Yet you tell me that I shouldn't give out information, that I should see a lawyer."

"*If* you're guilty."

"What else do you want to know, Mr. Lam?"

"Garvanza," I said. "Ever hear your husband mention that name?"

This time there could be no mistaking the little start that she gave; then her face was a poker face once more. "Garvanza," she said slowly. "I've heard that name somewhere."

"Your husband ever talk with you about a Garvanza?"

"No, I don't think he did. We discussed business very infrequently. I am not certain whether he knew a Mr. Garvanza or not."

I said, "When I mentioned Meredith, you wanted to know whether it was a man or a woman. On the Garvanza question you popped right out with a denial without asking whether it was Mr. Garvanza or Miss Garvanza or Mrs. Garvanza."

"Or the little Garvanza baby," she said sarcastically.

"Exactly."

"I'm very much afraid you and I aren't going to get along at all, Mr. Lam."

"I don't see any reason why not. I think we're doing fine."

"I don't."

"As soon as you get over the act of righteous indignation that you're using to cover up your slip when I mentioned Garvanza's name, I think we're going to be real chummy."

The slate-colored eyes studied me for four or five seconds which felt like as many minutes; then she said, "Yes, Mr. Lam. He knew Gabby Garvanza. I don't know how well. I've heard him speak of Mr. Garvanza, and when he read in the papers that Gabby Garvanza had been shot down in Los Angeles he was very, very much worried. I know that. He tried to keep me from seeing it, but I know that he was. Now I've answered your question. Where do we go from there?"

"Now," I said, "you're beginning to talk. Garvanza never called on him at the house here?"

"I have heard him mention Mr. Garvanza's name. And I know that he knew Gabby Garvanza. Offhand, I don't know exactly when Garvanza was shot. Let me see, that was on the Thursday before my husband disappeared. He was reading the paper, and all of a sudden he gave a startled exclamation, a half-strangled cry.

"It was at breakfast. I looked up at him and thought he might have something stuck in his throat. He coughed and reached for the coffee cup as though to take a swallow of liquid, then kept on coughing, putting on an act of having choked over something he'd eaten."

"What did you do?"

"I played right along. I got up and patted him on the back a few times, told him to hold his head down between his knees, and then, after a while, he quit coughing and smiled at me and said that a piece of toast had gone down his windpipe."

"You knew he was lying?"

"Of course."

"So what did you do?"

"After he'd left for the office I folded the newspaper

over in just the position it had been in when he'd been reading, and looked for the item that had alarmed him. It must have been the one about a Los Angeles mobster, Gabby Garvanza, being shot. I couldn't for the life of me figure out why that would have made any difference to George, but I remembered it. The paper said Garvanza would recover.

"I knew something was really bothering him all Sunday night and all Monday. When he told me he was going to the mine Tuesday I felt certain that in some way it had something to do with the thing that had been on his mind.

"You understand, Mr. Lam, I haven't any evidence for all this. It's simply womanly intuition, and I don't for the life of me know why I'm letting my hair down and telling you all this."

"Probably," I said, "because I called the turn and you *do* have a young lover. Therefore, you'd like very much to get the case cleared up before the police start messing around."

She said, "I don't know what it is about you, but you can say things and get away with them that would cause me to start slapping your face if it weren't for—for the way you say them. Sometimes—I don't know—you seem to be sincere."

"All right, you haven't answered the question."

"No, Mr. Lam. You're wrong. I haven't any lover, and I don't give a damn how much the police mess into my present."

"How about your past?"

Again her eyes held mine steadily. "That," she said, "I wouldn't like."

"Vulnerable?"

"I'm not answering questions on that. Anyway, I've given you all the information I have because I think you might be on the right track. While the police haven't started suspecting me as yet they will before very long, and I'd like to avoid that phase of the case. My husband took out insurance in my favor about six weeks ago."

"You haven't told the police that?"

"They haven't asked me."

I said, "Tell me about this mine up in Siskiyou County."

"It's owned by one of my husband's corporations. He had several different companies."

"Just where is this mine?"

"Somewhere up in the Seiad Valley. That's a wild country in the back part of Siskiyou County."

"What happens at the mine?"

She smiled. Her voice was that of a patient parent. "People work the mine. The ore is dumped into conveyors and carried down to the railroad. It's put aboard flat cars and shipped to the smelting company."

"That's another one of your husband's corporations?"

"He controls it, yes."

"And then what happens?"

"He gets checks from the smelting company for the amount of mineral that's in the ore."

"Big checks?"

"I think so. My husband makes big money."

"Who handles your husband's accounts? Does he have an office?"

"No, my husband has no office in the conventional sense of the word. He's a mining man. His office is under his hat. His accounts are kept by an income tax man—a Mr. Hartley L. Channing. You'll find him listed in the phone book."

"Know anything else that could be of help?"

She said, "There's one thing. My husband is terribly superstitious."

"In what way?"

"He is a great believer in luck."

"Most mining men are."

"But my husband has this one fixed superstition. No matter how many mines he opens and closes, one of them, usually the best one, must be named 'The Green Door,' and so carried on the books."

I thought that over. There was a gambling joint in San Francisco known as The Green Door. I wondered if she knew of that, and I wondered if her husband did. Perhaps he'd been lucky in the gambling house one night and felt the name would bring him luck in connection with his mining companies.

"Anything else?" I asked.

"Well, yes—in a way—"

"Go on."

"When my husband left Tuesday evening he knew that he was going into danger."

"How do you know?"

"He was always a little apprehensive about leaving me alone."

"Why?"

"I've tried to figure that one out, too. I think it's largely because he was an older man and I was so much younger and— Well, I think under those circumstances a man gets a little more possessive than would otherwise be the case, and is—shall we say, a little more apprehensive."

"So what?"

"So he made it a point to keep a gun in the bureau drawer. He had carefully instructed me how to use it."

"Go on."

"When he left Tuesday he took that gun with him. It was the first time he'd ever done that when he went on a trip."

"But he intended to drive all night?"

"A good part of the night."

"Then wouldn't it be natural for him to take the gun?"

"He'd driven all night lots of times before, but had never taken it. He'd always left it here for me."

"Did your husband tell you he was taking the gun?"

"No."

"How then do you know it was gone?"

"Because when I looked in the bureau drawer after he had left the gun wasn't there."

"It had been there before?"

"A couple of days before. I know that much."

"You don't know whether your husband was carrying it with him or whether he put it in a suitcase?"

"No."

"Now, you identified the contents of the suitcase?"

"Yes."

"How, when and where?"

"They took me to Petaluma. The car was being held there."

"It was your husband's car?"

"Yes."

"Where do the Berkeley police get in on it?"

She said, "Don't be silly. They're investigating all angles. If I'd had a young lover, as you suggested, and had conspired to kill George off, the conspiracy would have taken place here in this county and the lover would be here. Therefore, the Berkeley police are working on it. They're pretending that it's a matter of co-operation with the Sheriff of Sonoma County, but I've known all along what they were up to."

"Tell me about the suitcase."

"It was just exactly as I had packed it."

"You packed your husband's things?"

"That was one of the wifely duties I took over when I married him."

"How long have you been married?"

"About eight months."

"How did you happen to meet him?"

She smiled and shook her head.

"Was Bishop a widower?"

"No. There was a first Mrs. Bishop."

"What happened to her?"

"He bought her off."

"When?"

"After she began to—to get suspicious."

"There was a divorce?"

"Yes."

"A final decree?"

"Certainly. I tell you we're legally married."

"You wouldn't have taken a chance otherwise, would you?"

She looked me straight in the eyes. "Would you?"

"I don't know. I'm asking."

She said, "I have had my eyes open for a long time, and I went into this with my eyes open. I also went into it with the determination to play square in the event I got a square deal."

"Did you get a square deal?"

"I think I did."

"Do you ever get jealous?"

"No."

"Why not?"

"I don't think there's anything to get jealous about, and even if there were, I wouldn't run up my blood pressure over something you can't help, something that's—well, unavoidable."

"Okay," I said. "I'll see you later."

"How much later?"

"I don't know."

She said, "For your information I think the police will be having the house watched. They seem to think there's something pretty shady about the situation. They've handed me a good line and now they're going to keep a watch and see if George comes back home or if some other man should happen to come here."

"In that case," I said, "they've probably got me tagged already."

"Perhaps," she said.

"Your line will be tapped," I told her. "You say your husband's things were just the way you had packed them?"

"Yes."

"He hadn't unpacked a thing?"

"No."

"Then no one else had unpacked them?"

"What do you mean?"

"No one had searched the suitcase or the bag?"

"I don't think they had."

"Do the police have any idea you know what they're up to?"

"I can't tell."

"Have they questioned you—about your married life?"

"They've questioned me, but not about that."

"How much money did your husband carry with him?"

"He always carried several thousand dollars in a money belt."

"You don't know anything else that would help?"

"Nothing except what I've told you."

"Thanks," I said, and started for the door.

"You won't say anything about what I've told you—to the police—about Garvanza?"

I shook my head.

"After all, it's only a hunch, a vague suspicion."

"That's all."

"But somehow," she said, "I think I'm right."

"So do I," I told her, and walked out.

Chapter Twelve

It must have taken John Carver Billings the Second two days of concentrated thought to think up the alibi he had hired us to "discover."

It took the police less than two hours to bust that alibi wide open.

The last radio news of the evening announced that Los Angeles police, somewhat skeptical of young Billings's alibi in the Maurine Auburn murder case, had asked San Francisco police to check.

San Francisco police had checked.

The two girls who had been "located" by a private detective agency for John Carver Billings the Second had been sought by police.

One of the young women had purchased a new wardrobe and started on a vacation trip for South America. She was not immediately available. The other one, Sylvia Tucker, twenty-three, employed as a manicurist in a local barbershop, had at first sought to substantiate the alibi, but when police confronted her with proof that she had been in San Francisco on the Tuesday in question, she broke down and admitted that the whole alibi was phony, that she and her girlfriend had been well paid by the banker's son to concoct an alibi which would protect him for Tuesday night.

She claimed she didn't know why.

John Carver Billings the Second branded this as a brazen falsehood, an attempt on her part to get him into trouble, but from extraneous evidence police were convinced hers was the correct story and young Billings was caught in a trap of his own devising. John Carver Billings the Second, son of a well-known San Francisco financial figure, had therefore become the number-one suspect in the Maurine Auburn murder case.

I was in my pajamas preparatory to getting into bed in the stifling closeness of the cheap hotel bedroom, but after hearing the news broadcast I dressed, called a taxicab, and had it cruise past the Billings residence.

Lights were blazing. There were cars in front of the place. They were both police cars and newspaper cars. As I watched the place, from time to time I saw the lighted windows flare into brief oblongs of dazzling white light—newspaper reporters shooting pictures with synchronized flash guns.

I paid off the cab, took up a station in the shadows, and waited for an interminable interval until all the cars had left.

I didn't know whether there was a police shadow on the place or not. I had to take a chance. I prowled the back alley, got in through a garage, and tried the back door.

It was locked.

The blade of my penknife told me the key was in the lock. There was a good-sized crack under the back door. I had noticed a closet for preserved fruits on the back porch. I opened it and explored the shelves. They were lined with brown paper. I took out the jars of preserved fruit, took the stiff brown-paper lining from one of the shelves, slid this brown paper through the crack under the door, then punched out the key with the blade of my knife.

The key fell down on the paper. I gently slid the paper out from under the door, bringing the key with it.

I unlocked the back door, carefully replaced the key in the lock on the inside, replaced the brown paper on the shelf, put the preserves back into place, and quietly walked through the deserted kitchen toward the lighted part of the house.

There were no lights in the huge dining-room, but

beyond it in a library there were subdued lights and deep, comfortable chairs.

A door was open into a den behind the library. Two men were in there. I could hear low voices.

I stood for a moment and listened.

Evidently John Carver Billings the Second and his dad were holding a low-voiced conference.

I couldn't hear what they were saying and didn't try. A sudden impulse made me strive for the highly dramatic.

I sank down into one of the deep, high-backed reading-chairs that was turned partially away from the center of the room, and waited.

After a few minutes young Billings and his dad came back into the room.

I heard young Billings say something to his dad which I couldn't get. The father's reply was a monosyllable, then I caught the last words of Billings's closing sentence, ". . . that damn, double-crossing detective."

I said without moving, "I told you you were like a patient going to a doctor's office and ordering penicillin."

I couldn't see them but from the sudden silence I knew they were standing rigidly motionless; then I heard the father say, "Who was that? What kind of a trick is this?"

"You're in a jam," I told him. "Let's see if we can't do something about it."

They located my voice then.

The son ran around the table so that he could confront me.

"You damn crook!" he blazed.

I lit a cigarette.

Young Billings took a threatening step toward me. "Damn you, Lam. This much pleasure I'm going to have out of this situation. I'm going to—"

"Wait, John," his father said with a voice of quiet authority.

I said, "If you folks had put the cards on the table in the first place and asked us to clear you in the Bishop case, we'd have saved a lot of time."

Young Billings, who had been making with chest and fists, wilted like a punctured tire.

"What the devil do you mean about the Bishop case?" the father asked.

I said, "Bishop disappeared. Your son has been trying to get an alibi. The way I look at it, the answer has to be George Bishop. Now what do you want to tell me about it?"

"Nothing," young Billings said, recovering something of his poise. "How did you get in here?"

"I walked in."

"How?"

"Through the back door."

"That's a lie. The back door was locked."

"Not when I walked in," I told him.

"Take a look, John," the father said in a low, authoritative voice. "If it's unlocked, for heaven's sake lock it. We don't want any more people dropping in on us."

The son hesitated a moment, said, "I *know* it's locked, Dad."

"Make sure," the older man said crisply.

The son went out through the dining-room and the butler's pantry to the kitchen.

I said, "He's in a lot of trouble. Perhaps I could help him—if there's still time."

He started to say something to me, then thought better of it and waited.

After a moment, the son came back.

"Well?"

"The key's in the door, all right, Dad. I guess I must have neglected to turn it, but I certainly thought I locked that door after the servants left."

"I think we'd better have a talk, John," the father said.

"If Lam hadn't talked to the police we'd have been all right," John said. "We—"

"John!" the older man snapped crisply.

John ceased talking, as though his father's voice had been a whiplash.

There were several seconds of silence. I puffed away on the cigarette. Despite anything I could do my hand was trembling. I hoped no one noticed it. It was sink or swim now. If they called the police, I was all finished. This time it would be blackmail. They'd throw the book at me.

"I think you and I had better have a little talk, John," the father repeated, and led the way back to the den, leaving me sitting there.

I fought back a temptation to walk out. Now that the chips were in the center of the table I began to wonder if I held the right cards. If they decided to call the police, I was licked. If they didn't, I was going to have to start work on a case that had been so terribly, so hopelessly messed up that it was a thousand-to-one shot.

The comfortable overstuffed chair felt like the hot seat in the death house. Beads of perspiration kept forming on my forehead and hands. I was angry at myself because I couldn't control my nerves—but the perspiration kept coming just the same.

John Carver Billings the First came back and sat down in the chair opposite me. He said, "Lam, I think we are about ready to confide in you, provided one point can first be clarified."

"What is that?"

"We would want some assurance that the activity of the police in questioning the alibi of my son was not inspired by any action from your agency."

"Grow up," I said bitterly. "Your son went to considerable expense to try to establish an alibi. It was an alibi that was as flimsy as tissue paper. It wouldn't stand up. I knew it wouldn't stand up. He should have known it wouldn't stand up. I tried to find out why he wanted to establish that alibi and then give him some measure of decent protection rather than to rely on a fabrication which was all but self-evident.

"As a result, I've had five hundred dollars of our compensation taken from us. The police are searching for me as a blackmailer. My license as a detective may be revoked. My partner has become so frightened she's dissolved the partnership and instructed the bank to honor no more checks on the partnership account signed by me.

"That's what comes of my trying to give your boy something worthwhile instead of merely taking his money and calling it a day.

"Now, does that answer your question?"

John Carver Billings nodded his head in slow acquiescence. "Thank you, Mr. Lam, that answers my question."

I said, "You folks have wasted three or four days of time and probably several thousand dollars in cash. You've tried to extricate yourselves by methods that have backfired and left you in hot water. Now suppose we talk turkey?"

"What do *you* know about Bishop?" Billings asked.

"Not very much. I know most of what I know from reading the papers."

"There was nothing in the papers about us."

"Not in the papers," I said, "but you went to a lot of trouble to establish an alibi for last Tuesday night. The police know it. I know it. The question is, why? At first I thought the answer was a hit-and-run. Now I think it has to be more serious than that.

"There weren't any murders committed Tuesday night that the police *knew* about, so I started looking around to see if there might not have been one committed the police *didn't* know about."

"And you found?"

"I found George Bishop."

"You mean you've found him, you've found—"

"No," I interrupted. "Don't get me wrong. I unearthed the Bishop case. I went to see Mrs. Bishop about it."

"What did *she* say?"

"I questioned her as to whether there was a young lover in the picture, and whether she had deliberately planned her husband's murder. I felt that might have been where your son entered the picture. He couldn't afford scandal and he wanted the woman."

"What did she say?" the elder Billings asked.

"Just about what you'd expect."

"Perhaps what I'd expect and what you'd expect are two different things."

"Make it this way, then. Just about the answer that *I* expected."

"That doesn't mean a great deal to me," he said.

"And it didn't to me."

He paused to look me over pretty carefully, then said, "So now you're going to be cagey, eh?"

I said, "Try putting yourself in my position."

He thought that over.

"Let me question your son about Mrs. Bishop and see what he says."

"You're away off on the wrong track, Lam," he said.

At the moment, silence was my best weapon, so I sat silent.

Billings cleared his throat. "What I'm going to tell you, Lam, must be held in the *strictest* confidence."

I merely took a drag at the cigarette.

"This entire situation has become exceedingly embarrassing to me, personally," John Carver Billings said.

"That," I told him, "is a masterpiece of understatement. Exactly what happened Tuesday night?"

"I have no firsthand knowledge of that. I got the information from my son."

"What information?"

"We have a yacht," he said, "a rather pretentious, sixty-
five-foot cabin cruiser. We call it the *Billingboy* and it is
moored at one of the exclusive yacht clubs here in the
bay."

"Go on."

"Tuesday, my son persuaded Sylvia Tucker, a young
woman who has been a passing fancy—an attractive manicurist—to ring up the place where she works and say she
had a headache and couldn't come to work. Then she went
out in the boat with my son.

"They were together all day Tuesday until about four
o'clock in the afternoon when they returned from their
outing, and my son took her to her apartment.

"Then my boy had a few drinks and left her there. He
knew that I didn't approve either of Sylvia or of the idea of
trips of this sort, and I think he rather dreaded meeting me.

"So he stopped in several places for drinks with which
to nerve himself; then argued himself into believing that
he could cover things up so I need never know he had
used the yacht.

"With that in mind he went down to the yacht planning
on changing his clothes and fixing things so it would seem
he had spent the biggest part of the day working on the
boat.

"Now, in order to definitely understand what followed,
Mr. Lam, it's going to be necessary to explain something of
the nature of the yacht club."

"Go ahead and explain it."

"The club is so situated that we could very easily be
plagued with sightseers and, of course, we don't want to
have the general public climbing around over boats. They
do not understand, or do not appreciate, the care that

should be given a boat. Nails in the heels of shoes, for instance, would work irreparable injury upon the highly varnished decks of an expensive yacht."

I said, "You're trying to tell me that the yacht club is carefully closed off so that the public is excluded?"

"Exactly."

"What else?"

"There is a high fence running on the land side, a fence topped with barbed wire, and so arranged that it would be virtually impossible for anyone to climb over the fence. The top three strands of barbed wire are on posts at an angle to the meshed wire so that they make an overhang. No one could climb the fence and get in over the top."

I nodded. "Go ahead."

"There is but one gate. There is always a watchman on duty to check the persons who come in and the persons who go out. That is intended both as a safeguard and so the caretaker will know who is actually present at the club at any particular time in case telephone calls should be received."

"In other words, whenever you go into the yacht club the attendant marks down the fact that you are there?"

"The time of arrival and the time of departure in a book which is kept for that purpose, just as one registers in an office building after hours."

"Isn't that rather embarrassing at times?"

"Perhaps with a club that had more of a rowdy membership it might be, but this is a very conservative club. Members who are inclined to throw wild parties on their yachts find it expedient to join some other club which has more lax standards."

"All right, go ahead. What happened?"

"Now, to get back to this Tuesday evening. My son went down to the yacht, planning to arrange things so I would think he had been working on it all day, and therefore when he found that the watchman at the gate was engrossed for the moment in a telephone conversation, with his back turned, it seemed like a providential opportunity, so my son slipped on through the gate. There is an electric connection so an electric buzzer sounds whenever one starts down the ramp to the mooring-float. For some reason this was not working at the moment. My son went down to the yacht. No one saw him. No one knows he was there. No one can ever prove he was there. You must at all times remember that, Mr. Lam."

"All right, then what?"

"When my son boarded the yacht, unlocked the door, and entered the main cabin he found—well, he found himself in a very grave predicament."

"What sort of predicament?"

"The body of George Tustin Bishop was lying on the floor. He had been shot, and apparently the killing had taken place within an hour or so of the time my son boarded the yacht."

I digested that information. The sweating started again. My palms were once more moist. I was in it now, all right. A nice murder, and I was tied up with the Billings boy, fake alibi and all.

"My son reached a decision," Billings went on. "It was not a commendable decision, but, nevertheless, having reached it, it was irrevocable and we must deal with it as an accepted fact."

My silence showed him how I felt about that.

"In order to understand the circumstances," Billings went on, hastily, apologetically, "you must realize that my son felt that I might have been involved in the matter."

"In what way?"

"There had been some trouble with Bishop."

"What was the nature of that trouble?"

"It was a financial matter."

"You owed him money?"

"Good heavens, no, Mr. Lam. I owe money to no man."

"What was the nature of the trouble, then?"

"Bishop was a promoter, a mining promoter."

"He owed you money?"

"Yes, but that was not the issue; that is, he owed the bank money. Not individually, but as a majority stockholder of the Skyhook Mining and Development Syndicate."

"Go ahead."

"I'm afraid all of the details would take too much time."

"Go ahead. Tell me. We have time now. Later on, we may not have it."

"Well, it's a long story."

"Give me the highlights."

"Bishop was a peculiar character. He was a very heavy individual depositor in the bank of which I am president. In addition to that he had huge interests in various mining development companies, the nature of which we do not clearly understand. In fact, as we begin to investigate his mining activities, they become more and more mysterious."

"What about the money he owed you?"

"Well, as I mentioned, he has perhaps a dozen various companies in which he holds apparently the controlling interest, but where stock is offered to the public."

"With the permission of the corporation commission?"

"Oh, of course. He gets permission to sell the stock. They are listed as highly speculative stocks and there are ample safeguards to see that the promoters do not make the money at the expense of the public. However, now that the bank has started an investigation we find that there is a certain peculiar overall pattern in connection with these corporations."

"What?"

"They are formed; money is borrowed at the bank for development. A certain amount of development work is done, and then the mine has a tendency to become inactive and—"

"What about the loans?"

"The loans are paid off promptly when they become due."

"What about the stockholders?"

"That is the peculiar thing, Mr. Lam. It is something I cannot understand."

"Go ahead."

"A certain amount of stock is sold to the public; not a great amount. Most of that stock is held in escrow. Then apparently—and you understand I didn't know this until the last forty-eight hours when our investigators reported—the stock is bought up by someone who pays the stockholders just about what they paid for the stock."

"Suppose the stockholders don't want to sell?"

"The stock that is not sold back—"

"Wait a minute, you say 'back.' What do you mean by that?"

"We have every reason to believe that the person who buys the stock is the representative of George Tustin Bishop."

"All right. What about the people who don't want to sell?"

"They're permitted to hold their stock for another six months or a year, and then an offer is resumed. Eventually they either sell the stock or it becomes valueless. The mine languishes with no further development work being done."

"Now, what," I asked, "would be the idea of making a wash transaction of that sort? There must be considerable overhead."

"There is. Not only are there legal expenses, but there

is the selling commission. There is, however, no great drive to sell the stock. A prospectus is put out and the stock is sold in every instance entirely by mail. After a small percentage has been sold, selling activities are discontinued. Then the corporation goes through a quiescent period, after which the stock is bought back."

"It doesn't make sense," I said.

"Exactly."

"All right, tell me about this Skyhook Mining and Development Syndicate."

"Now, there we have a very peculiar situation. The organization of that corporation apparently followed the usual pattern. Permission was given to sell the stock at par value, allowing a fifteen-percent commission for the salesmen, but with the understanding that all of the balance of the money must go into the treasury of the corporation, and that there could be no disbursements until certain prerequisites in the nature of development work had been done."

"How was the money secured for the development work?"

"The understanding of the corporation commission was that the sales of the stock would be handled by a syndicate, and that the fifteen percent, together with contributions made in the form of a loan by the organizers, would go toward the initial development."

"So that the stockholders would be getting a free ride?"

"If you want to put it that way, yes."

"And that was done?"

"That was done. The corporation was permitted to endorse a note, which was signed by George Tustin Bishop, with the understanding that every penny of the proceeds would go into the treasury of the corporation."

"How much was the note?"

"Twenty-five thousand dollars."

"Then what happened?"

"Then a peculiar thing happened. Something about the name appealed to the investing public. I understand the solicitation was by mail, but the public reacted very favorably. The records indicate that some fifty percent of the treasury stock was sold to the public under the conditions laid down by the commissioner of corporations."

"That was a departure from the usual pattern of the Bishop corporations?"

"Yes, sir. Very much so."

"And then what happened?"

"Then," Billings said, "Bishop flatly refused to meet the note. He drew out every cent of money he had in our bank and stated he had no funds with which to meet that note, and that we would necessarily call upon the corporation as an endorser to make good the amount of the loan."

"What had happened to the money in the treasury of the corporation?"

"It had been spent for development work. Now, then, Mr. Lam, I dislike very much to go into this because it is something that would ruin us if it became public."

"What?"

"The bank made a very extensive investigation through certain channels which are open to a bank, which would not be open to the general public, and concerning which I do not want to make any statements."

"All right, what was the result of the investigations?"

"Ore was being shipped from the Skyhook mine and sent in flat cars to the George T. Bishop Smelting Corporation."

"Then what happened?"

"Then comes the incredible part of the whole thing," Billings said. "The ore was being smashed up into fine particles and used to grade roads, for earth fills, and used as ballast."

"Ore was shipped down out of the mountains, smashed up, and then transported by freight to wind up as mere crushed rock?"

"Exactly."

I said, "There must be a mistake somewhere."

"There is no mistake. We have found that the same procedure was followed in virtually every one of the mines where any development work was done. Ore was shipped down to the smelting and refining company, and by the smelting and refining company was converted into road ballast."

"In other words, Bishop was a swindler."

"I'm not making that as a flat accusation. Certainly there is something going on that is definitely far from the normal development of a business venture."

"What would the smelting company pay for this ore which it converted into road ballast?"

"Various amounts," Billings said, "until the mining corporation had received enough to repay the loan which it had made; then the mining company became inactive, there were no further shipments of ore, the loan was paid, and the company was virtually dissolved, with nearly all of the stockholders exercising the option which had been given them by the commissioner of corporations to withdraw the amount of money which had been put in for their stock and had been held in escrow for a period of a year."

"You went to the commissioner of corporations, of course?"

"No, sir. I did not."

"Why?"

"Because the bank was involved in the transaction to a certain extent. Perhaps we should have exercised a closer scrutiny over the affairs of these corporations, but because Mr. Bishop customarily kept a very large balance in our bank, and because his various accounts were quite active, we took him at face value."

"But when you found out—then what?"

"We asked for an explanation from Mr. Bishop."

"Did you let him know what you had found out?"

"We found out a lot of this after—well, too late. But Bishop knew we were making the investigation."

"You had found out *some* of this before Tuesday?"

"Yes. By last Tuesday we knew enough to put us very much on guard, to make us rather suspicious."

"And you had asked Bishop to meet with you and explain matters?"

"Yes."

"You had asked him to meet with you when?"

Billings coughed.

"When?"

"On Tuesday night."

"Where?"

"At my house."

"All right. Now let's go back to the boat. Your son found Bishop's body on the boat. What did he do?"

"He realized that fortuitously no one knew he was aboard the yacht."

"What time was all this?"

"It was well after dark."

"So what did he do?"

"He undressed. You see, we each of us have a state-room on the yacht and each stateroom has a closet containing a lot of clothes. Therefore my son was able to divest himself of his entire wearing-apparel without creating any attention."

"Then what?"

"Then he put on a pair of bathing trunks, put the key to the automobile in the pocket of his bathing trunks, locked up the yacht, slipped over the side, and swam out into the channel. Then, swimming quietly, he rounded the premises of the yacht club and managed to gain one of the bathing beaches, where he came ashore, apparently a man who had merely been out for an evening swim. He walked boldly past the few people who were, for the most part, sitting in parked automobiles looking out over the water, and went to the place where he had left his car. He used the key to turn on the ignition. He came home, took a shower, dried out his wet bathing-suit, and put on his clothes."

"Then what?"

"I had been out at a business conference and unfortunately he had to wait for me to come home."

"Go on."

"It was almost eleven o'clock when I arrived."

"So what did you do?"

"My son told me what had happened. I warned him that he had made a very poor decision, that he should have notified the police immediately."

"I presume then that you called the police?"

"Not the police. I decided to let the caretaker at the yacht club discover the body."

"So what did you do?"

"I called the caretaker and asked him to go aboard my yacht and get a briefcase which was in the main cabin and send it to me by taxicab."

"What happened?"

"I presumed, of course, that when he went to the main cabin he would find the body and report to the police."

"He didn't do so?"

"The body wasn't there."

"How do you know?"

"The night watchman sent me the briefcase by taxicab, just as I had instructed him. That caused me grave concern. I questioned my son very carefully to see if there was any chance he had been aboard another yacht, or if he had imagined any of the things he had found. Then the next morning I personally went down and boarded the yacht and made an inspection."

"What did you find?"

"There was no indication that there had ever been a body in the cabin of the yacht. No one was there. Things were just as I had left them."

"How did the night watchman get aboard the yacht?"

"He has a key. It is not mandatory that owners leave extra keys in the safe at the yacht club, but the management prefers to have them do so. Then, in case of fire, or in case of any urgent necessity, the caretakers can get aboard the yachts and move them."

"Then what happened?"

"My son was worried because we didn't know just what *had* happened. He decided it would be a good plan for him to have an alibi for Tuesday night."

"*You* had one?"

"Oh, yes. I was in conference with a business associate. One of the directors of the bank."

"Give me his name and address."

"Surely, Mr. Lam, you don't doubt my—"

"I'm not doubting. I'm investigating. What's his name and address?"

"Waldo W. Jefferson. He's one of the directors of the bank. He has offices in the bank building."

"How about guests that go aboard yachts?" I asked. "Are they registered?"

"No, just the owner registers, but the number of guests is noted. That is, the registration will show that the owner boarded the yacht, that he had two guests, three guests, four guests, or whatever the case might have been."

I said, "All right, let's go down to the yacht. You can register me as a guest."

"But I have already gone through the yacht carefully,

Mr. Lam. There's no evidence there that—"

"Perhaps no evidence that you can see, but if the body of a dead man was once aboard your yacht and the police have any reason to suspect that such was the case, you're apt to find there's a lot of evidence they'll uncover which you never knew existed."

An expression of smug satisfaction flitted across his face. "There is nothing, Mr. Lam."

"Perhaps."

"Just what do you expect to find, Mr. Lam? What do you want to look for?"

I said, "I once attended one of Frances G. Lee's seminars on homicide investigation."

"I dare say you have proper professional qualifications, Mr. Lam. I fail to see why we should discuss them at this time, however."

I went on as though there had been no interruption. "They called for a volunteer to take off his coat and roll up his sleeves. They had a test tube of human blood. They put blood smears on his hands and arms."

"There have been no blood smears on my hands or arms," he said with dignity.

"And then," I said, "they told him to go wash the blood off, to use soap and water, to scrub, to do everything he could to get rid of the bloodstains."

"Well, it washed right off, didn't it?"

"Sure."

"Then what?"

"Nothing," I said.

"What do you mean, nothing?"

"They went on with the class."

"You mean they simply had him put the blood on and then wash it off?"

"That's right."

"I don't see your point, Lam."

"Then the next day they asked him if he'd taken a bath, and he said he had. They asked him if he'd scrubbed his hands and arms particularly well—devoting an unusual amount of attention to them—and he admitted that he had, that he felt they might be going to play some trick on him so he'd made a good job of it."

"Then what?"

"Nothing."

"Lam, what are you getting at?"

"The next day they did the same thing," I said.

"He'd taken another bath?"

"Yes."

"And scrubbed his hands and arms?"

"Yes."

"Well, Lam, I don't see what you're getting at. You're creating a divergence and—"

"And then," I said, "they rolled up his sleeves, put on a reagent, and every place where the blood had touched his arms there was a dark-blue stain."

John Carver Billings sat as perfectly quiet as a mouse on a pantry shelf when a door opens. I could see him digesting that information and he didn't like it.

Abruptly he straightened in his chair, said in that calm, precise, close-clipped banker's voice of his, "Very well, Mr. Lam, we will now go to the yacht."

Chapter Thirteen

Floating palaces of teakwood and mahogany, glistening with varnish, dotted with polished brass, rocked quietly at their moorings, waiting patiently for the weekends when their owners would take them out for a few hours' recreation on the waters of the bay, or, perhaps in the case of the more venturesome, out into the pounding whitecaps beyond the heads and through to the long rollers of the surging ocean.

Some of them were so large they would require a crew to operate them; others were of a modern construction with controls so ingeniously arranged that one man could, in case of necessity, handle the boat.

It was as Billings had told me. The yacht club was virtually inaccessible to any but members. The high, steel-meshed fence was surmounted with an inclined barrier of heavy barbed wire, and at the gate there was a balanced platform. When we stepped on that a buzzer sounded, and the night gateman who was on duty gave Billings a respectful "Good evening, sir," and handed him a book. Billings wrote his name, and, in a separate column next to the name, added the information, *One guest*. The watchman checked the time.

He wanted to say something else, but Billings cut him off with a curt "Some other time, Bob," and piloted me down the long inclined ramp to the floats where we could hear the gentle lap of water and see the shimmering reflection of lights.

Our feet on the float gave back booming echoes from the water below. There was a grim, eerie atmosphere clinging to the place. Neither one of us said anything.

We came to a trim white hull surmounted by teakwood and brass. The upper cabin had square windows of heavy plate glass. There was a line of conventional round ports on the lower level.

"This is it," Billings said. "Please keep on the mat and don't step on the deck with those shoes. I'll open up the cabin."

We climbed aboard. Billings fitted a key to a padlock. A sliding panel opened up a companionway where rubber treads were bound with glistening brass. A light switch flooded a cabin into brilliance.

"It was here," Billings said.

I soaked up the luxurious atmosphere of the cabin. It fairly reeked with money.

My feet moved over the carpet. I might have been walking on thick moss in a virgin forest. The color scheme of that cabin had been carefully carried out even to the last thread. Expensive draperies masked the interior of the cabin from the curious outer world. Chairs, books, a fine radio—every creature comfort that could possibly be packed into the confines of a yacht's cabin.

"Where was the body?" I asked.

"As nearly as I can gather from what my son told me, it was lying here. You see, there isn't the faintest stain in the carpet." I got down on my hands and knees.

"You don't need to do that," he said. "There isn't the faintest stain in the carpet."

I kept crawling around. I saw that Billings was getting irritated.

"Not even the *faintest* stain in the carpet," I agreed with him at length.

"You could have taken my word for that," he said.

"There isn't any stain in the carpet," I went on, "because the carpet is brand new and has only recently been installed."

"What the devil are you talking about?" he demanded. "This carpet has been here ever since—"

I shook my head and moved one of the chairs about an inch. The place where the legs of the chair had made an indentation in the deep carpet were plainly visible.

"The carpet," I said, "has been here ever since the chair was placed there."

"This is a very fine carpet. It returns to its original position very rapidly. You will find that—"

"I know," I said, "but it's impossible to completely eliminate the marks of the chairs. You'll notice this same thing about every one of the chairs. What's more, you'll notice there's a photograph of you sitting in the cabin, reading." I indicated a framed photograph. "You can't tell the color of the carpet from that picture, but you certainly can see the pattern. It isn't this one."

There was dismay on his face as he looked at the picture.

I walked around the cabin, looking in the dark corners, running my fingers around inaccessible places.

"You'll notice right here, Mr. Billings, there's a very faint smear here where something has been wiped with what evidently was a damp rag and— Wait a minute, what's this?"

"What?"

"Over here in the corner, about two feet up," I said.

"I hadn't noticed it," he told me, bending down.

"I'm satisfied you haven't, but you'd better notice it now."

"What is it?"

I said, "It's a small, round hole with a very peculiar dark ring around the outer perimeter. It's about the size of a thirty-eight-caliber bullet, and there's a very, very faint reddish-brown streak here which looks as though it might be a piece of animal tissue which was adhering to the bullet and which was carried partially into the hole made by the bullet."

John Carver Billings looked at me in silence.

"And now," I went on casually, "if, as you said, you had an appointment with Bishop for Tuesday night at your house, how did it happen you went over to spend the evening with Mr. Waldo W. Jefferson? *How did you know Mr. Bishop wasn't going to be able to keep his appointment at your house?*"

Billings looked as though I'd thrown a bucket of cold salt water in his face. He gave one gasp, then simply stood there, jaw sagging.

And in that instant I became conscious of sound.

It was a peculiar pounding sound, as though made by many feet. Very plainly the hum of voices became audible, voices which seemed to be right outside the yacht, but which were muffled by the walls of the cabin so that they registered only as undertones of rumbling conversation in heavy masculine voices.

John Carver Billings climbed the steps and slid back the hatch. "Who are *you*?" a voice asked.

Before Billings had a chance to answer, I heard the voice of the gateman saying, "That's Mr. Billings, sir. John Carver Billings. He came aboard just a few moments before you arrived."

"Going some place, buddy?" a heavy voice asked.

"Mr. John Carver Billings, the banker," the watchman's voice said.

The heavy voice said, "Oh." The tone was deferential.

Steps moved on. The watchman remained behind to explain. "There's been a bit of trouble, sir. I wanted to tell you about it but you didn't have the time to listen. There seems to have been a body found aboard the *Effie A.* The night watchman was attracted by a very evident disagreeable odor. The owner of the boat, you know, is away on a vacation. It seems that someone forced the lock and— I'm afraid it's going to make for a nasty bit of publicity, sir, but there was nothing the club could do except notify the police."

"I see," Billings said. "The owner of the boat isn't here?"

"No, sir. He's on a trip to Europe. The boat's been closed up and—"

"No one's borrowed it?"

"No, sir. No one."

John Carver Billings said impatiently, "Well, go ahead, don't let me interfere. See that the police are given every assistance." He slammed the sliding panel shut and came back down to the cabin.

His skin was the color of stale library paste. He avoided my eyes.

I said, "I'm going to have to do a lot of work and I'm going to have to do it fast. I want some money."

He pulled a wallet from his pocket, opened it, and started taking out hundred-dollar bills.

I said, "Your son stopped payment of a check that was given the partnership in Los Angeles, and—"

"I'm very, very sorry about that. That's a matter which will be rectified at once, Mr. Lam. I'll instruct the bank to—"

"Don't instruct the bank to do anything," I said. "Payment of the check was stopped. Let it stay that way. But you can add five hundred dollars to what you're giving me as expense money."

"Expense money?"

"That's right. There's going to be a hell of a lot of expenses. You can add the five hundred dollars onto the other."

He merely nodded and kept on dishing out folding money.

Looking at the size of the wallet I knew then that he'd carefully prepared for just such an emergency. This was getaway money, and there was a terrific wad of it. That, the bullet hole in the yacht, and the new carpet told me just about all I needed to know.

Chapter Fourteen

I'd once done a favor for this broker, a favor he couldn't very well forget, so when I called him at eight o'clock in the morning he was eager to see that my business received top priority.

I said, "I have thirteen hundred and fifty dollars in cash."

"Yes, Lam."

"I want you to invest three hundred and fifty dollars in stock of the Skyhook Mining and Development Syndicate."

"Never heard of it, Lam."

"Find out about it, hear about it. Locate the stock. I want it. I want it fast."

"Yes. And the other thousand dollars?"

"The three hundred and fifty dollars," I said, "goes in the name of Elsie Brand. I want one thousand dollars invested in the same stock and that will be in the name of Cool and Lam, a copartnership. I want you to locate that stock, and I want you to buy it the first thing this morning, and—"

"Wait a minute," he said. "I'm looking through a card index now— Wait a minute, here it is. That was one of those mail-order promotion things, Lam. It may take a little while to find out who the stockholders are, and—"

"There isn't that much time," I said. "It cleared through the corporation commission. The stock had to be placed in escrow for a year, during which time the purchasers of stock could back out if they wanted to, and during the year certain development work had to be made, otherwise the sales were invalid at the option of the purchaser."

"Well?"

I said, "Get in touch with the escrow holder. Say that

you're in a position to offer his clients a reasonable profit, and that you're looking for information. Don't tell him who for or what. Tell him you can get that information either the easy way or the hard way. Then start working on the long-distance telephone and buy up stock."

"How high shall I go?"

"Up to twice the par value. If you can't get it for that, quit. And remember, there's a note of the corporation that's outstanding. The bank hasn't done anything about it because Bishop was on that note. Now he's dead, they'll have to do something about it. The escrow holder should know that. The stockholders should know it. If they don't, see that they do."

"All right," he promised. "I'll get busy."

"Real busy," I insisted.

"Right now."

I went back to the morning newspapers. They featured the story in big headlines.

Mining Man's Body Found on Millionaire's Yacht.

It was a natural, and the crime reporters really went to town on it.

Erickson B. Payne, the bachelor millionaire owner of the yacht, was on a vacation in Europe. There could be no question but that he had been out of the United States for the past four weeks, and, aside from the one duplicate key which was kept in the safe at the yacht club, there were no keys to his yacht. However, the police investigation disclosed that the padlock on the boat had evidently been smashed, and a new padlock had then been placed on the yacht so that the night watchman, in making his rounds, would not notice anything unusual.

Police acted on the theory that the mining man had been murdered at some other point and the body had then been transported to the yacht club, but how the body could have reached the yacht club was a major mystery.

I read the accounts for the third time while I waited in the office of Hartley L. Channing.

It was a nice office, with his name on the frosted glass, *Hartley L. Channing, Accounting*. There was a nice receptionist who looked cool and comfortable, but very cute, with a peaches-and-cream complexion and wide, blue eyes.

She had been reading a magazine when I entered the office. It was a magazine that was concealed in a desk drawer which she closed, and when I announced I would wait for Mr. Channing, she wearily opened another drawer, pulled out paper, which she ratcheted in the machine, and started a laborious job of copy work, clacking the keys of the typewriter with mechanical precision but without any particular enthusiasm.

It had been five minutes past nine when I entered the place and the girl typed steadily for fifteen minutes.

Hartley Channing came in promptly at nine-twenty.

"Hello," he said to me. "What can I do for you?"

"My name's Lam. I want to talk about some tax work."

"Very well. Come on in."

He ushered me into his private office.

The clacking of the typewriter stopped as soon as I had crossed the threshold.

"Sit down, Lam. What can I do for you?"

He was a breezy individual, well dressed, well groomed, with fingernails that had been manicured within the last couple of days, an expensive hand-painted cravat, a fine tailor-made suit of imported worsted, and shoes that looked as though they could have been custom-made.

I said, "You handled Mr. Bishop's work, didn't you?"

His eyes instantly slipped colorless curtains between us. "Yes," he said, and volunteered no more information.

"Too bad about him."

"I understand there's some mystery."

"Seen the morning papers?"

"No," he said, and I knew right then he was lying. "I've been busy on another matter and—"

"There isn't any mystery about him any more."

"What do you mean?"

"The body was found aboard a yacht in one of the yacht clubs."

"He's dead, then?"

"Yes."

"His death is definitely established?"

"Yes."

"How did he die?"

"Two bullet wounds. One bullet in the body and one bullet which went entirely through the head."

"Too bad. I'm very sorry to hear it. However, you had some matters you wanted to consult me about?"

"A tax matter."

"What's the nature of it, Mr. Lam?"

"I want to know how much you know about the flim-flam that Bishop was running."

"What do you mean, sir?"

"If you kept his books and tax affairs you know exactly what I mean."

"I don't like your attitude, Mr. Lam. May I ask if this is official?"

"It's not official. It's personal and friendly."

"Who are you?"

"I'm a detective from Los Angeles, a private detective."

"I don't think I have anything to discuss with you, Lam."

I said, "Look, buddy, the chips are down. Now let's quit fooling around with this thing. You're mixed up in it. I want to know how deep."

"I am quite certain I don't know what you're talking about, Lam, and I don't like the way you talk. I'm going to have to ask you to leave."

I said, "Bishop had a lot of activities. He was smart. He decided he'd report the income but he wouldn't divulge the *source* of that income. So he engaged in a lot of mining activities that were a complete hoax."

"Bishop never swindled a man in his life."

"Of course he didn't. He was too careful for that. If he'd done that he'd have been arrested, complaint would have been made to the corporation commissioner, and he'd have been out of business. He didn't swindle anyone. He simply swapped dollars with himself. He had a lot of companies and he reported income to those companies and then he juggled funds and stock around so that nobody could tell just who was doing what. However, he was very careful to keep his nose clean on actually reporting the income. The thing he didn't want to report was the *source* of the income. Now, looking at it from my standpoint, there's just one answer to that."

Channing picked up a pencil and began to fiddle with it nervously. "I am quite certain that I don't care to discuss Mr. Bishop's affairs with anyone who isn't directly interested, or fully authorized."

I said,, "You're going to discuss them with me and then you're going to discuss them with the police. You may not know it, buddy, but you're in a jam."

"You've intimated that several times, Lam, and I've told you that I don't like it. I keep liking it less all the time." He pushed back his chair and got to his feet.

He was a big, athletic-looking chap, a little heavy around the waist, but there was also a lot of weight in his shoulders.

"Get out," he said, "and stay out."

I said, "Bishop was planning a fast move. He wouldn't have planned it without consulting with you, and as I size you up you wouldn't have gone along on a business of this sort on a salary basis. I think you have a finger in the pie."

"All right," he said, "here's the end of the line for you. You're going to get hurt now."

He came round the desk.

I sat perfectly still.

"Get going," he said, and grabbed me by the coat collar with his left hand.

"Up."

He jabbed a thumb under my chin.

He'd been around, that boy. He knew the exact nerve centers where a jabbing thumb would bring a man up out of a chair.

I got up out of the chair fast. He spun me around toward the door.

"You've asked for this," he said. "Now you're going to take your medicine like a little man."

He swung me out at arm's length and reached for the knob of the entrance door.

The knob made noise, and immediately on the other side of the door I heard the keys start rattling once more on the typewriter.

I said, "You may have an alibi on Bishop's murder. You may not. But that doesn't mean you have one on Maurine Auburn, and Gabby Garvanza isn't going to be easy. When I tell him—"

The hand dropped away from the doorknob as though the arm had wilted.

For a long moment he stood there, absolutely motionless, watching me with cold, blue eyes that held no more emotion than the keys on an adding-machine. Then he let go of me, walked completely around the desk, settled himself, picked up the pencil again, and said, "Sit down, *Mister* Lam."

I said, "If you want to save yourself a lot of trouble, start talking."

"You can tell Gabby that I don't know a thing about

Maurine, and that's the honest truth."

I said, "It isn't healthy to get in Gabby's way."

"I'm not in his way."

He shot out his cuff nervously, picked up the pencil, twisted it in his fingers, then reached for his handkerchief, blew his nose, wiped his forehead, put his handkerchief back in his pocket, and cleared his throat.

I said, "Start talking."

"I know nothing about Maurine."

"Can you make a judge believe that?"

"To hell with a judge. What does he have to do with it?"

I smiled at him, a gloating smile of cold triumph. "If you get in Gabby's way and he can frame you for a murder, he's going to do it, and let the state take care of you, and you know that as well as I do."

The guy's coat retained its tailor-made lines, but the body inside of the coat had shrunk and slumped. The coat looked two sizes too large.

"Now, look," he said, "you're working for Gabby Garvanza and—"

"I didn't tell you for whom I was working," I interrupted.

I saw his eyes widen. There was an expression of incipient relief.

"But," I said, "I now have some information Gabby Garvanza is going to want. And I want to know about Bishop. Now start talking."

That did it. The crack about Gabby framing a murder on him had taken all the starch out of his spine and he was too terror-stricken to think clearly, to even try to figure out my real interest. He had hypnotized himself into static terror.

He said, "All I know about is the bookkeeping. We fixed it so that every bit of income Bishop had came from those mining companies."

"And the mining companies?" I asked.

"Among their various activities," he said, "they oper-ated The Green Door. There was nothing in their charters that said they couldn't. No reason why a company can't operate anything it wants.

"Now, I can tell you this much. When Gabby Garvanza wanted to move into San Francisco, some of the fellows decided they would make it tough for him, but that wasn't Bishop's idea. Bishop and I wanted to play ball with him all along. If he could furnish the protection we were willing to pay for that protection. We didn't care where the money went to or who got it. All we wanted was the commodity. We were willing to buy it from the one who could give us the best service.

"Now, that's the truth, Mr. Lam. I never did buck Gabby and neither did Bishop."

I said, "How well did you know Maurine?"

"You know how well I knew her—at least Gabby does. I introduced Maurine to him. I knew her well. Bishop knew her damn well."

"And what about Mrs. Bishop?" I asked.

"Irene keeps out of the business."

I said, "I want her background."

"Don't you know?"

"No."

He tried to get control of himself and almost made it. "If you're in with Gabby Garvanza there's a lot you don't know."

"And a lot I do. I have some *very* interesting informa-tion for Gabby. Now tell me about Irene."

For some reason the guy was scared half to death of Gabby. My walking in and asking him about Maurine had jarred him right down to the shoelaces.

He said, "Irene was in burlesque. She was a striptease artist. Bishop went out on a party with her one night and

they clicked. He fell for her like a ton of bricks and she—
Well, she played her cards smart as hell."

"Was it a legal wedding?"

"Legal? You're damn right it was legal. Irene saw to
that. She had the smartest lawyer in town handle the
whole thing. She insisted on a legal marriage. He had to
buy his wife out. Irene may look dumb but she's smart."

"Who killed Maurine Auburn?"

"I swear that I don't know, Lam. I tell you honestly I
don't know. I was absolutely, utterly shocked by it. I—I
liked her."

"Who killed Bishop?"

"I don't know. I wish I did. Put yourself in my place. I
don't know where *I* stand. For all I know someone may be
trying to put the finger on me. That's not a nice feeling.

"You can tell Gabby that I want to see him. I've been
trying to reach him. He can help me."

I sneered at him.

He mopped his face again.

"What's going to happen to The Green Door now?"

"There'll be no opposition as far as I'm concerned to
anything Gabby wants to do. Provided, of course, he can
fix it up with the others, and— Well, I guess he can."

"What do you know about John Carver Billings?"

"Billings is all right. He's the banker. We use him occa-
sionally. He doesn't ask any questions just so we keep a
good balance in his bank."

"Does he know any questions to ask?"

"I don't think so. George had a stranglehold on him
because of the boy."

"What's all this business about wanting him to foreclose
on the Skyhook Mining and Development Syndicate?"

"Now, there," Channing said, "you've got me. I told
George a hundred times that that was the most foolish
thing he could do. It was apt to result in an investigation.

It might even ruin the entire business structure."

"He didn't listen to you?"

"No. He wanted that foreclosure filed. He said he didn't give a damn what happened, he wanted the foreclosure filed. Tell Gabby I'd like to talk with him—any time."

"How about the widow?"

He laughed. "What does *she* have to do with it?"

"She might have a great deal."

Channing said, "Make no mistake about this, Mr. Lam. You can tell Gabby Garvanza I am taking over The Green Door."

"What will Irene get out of it?"

"Irene," he said, "will share in the estate. She was a damn good burlesque stripper. She had what it takes and she gave what she had, but she's small potatoes. She got hers and now she's out of it. As of tonight I'm taking over."

Some of his assurance began to come back.

"And the corporations?"

"The corporations will be all washed up in a smother of figures."

I said, "Stay right here until two o'clock in the afternoon. Don't go out under any circumstances and don't give anyone any definite information. If Gabby wants to see you he'll tell you where you can contact him."

That frightened him again. The thought of walking into Gabby's clutches didn't appeal to him at all.

"Tell him to phone me."

"I thought you wanted to see him."

"I do, but I'm going to be terribly busy. Now that it's established that George is dead, the police will be here, and—"

"I thought you wanted to see Gabby."

"I do, I do, but I have other things."

"Shall I tell Gabby you're too busy to see him?"

"No! No! I didn't mean it that way."

"It sounded that way."

"Just put yourself in my position, Lam."

"I sure as hell wouldn't want to do that," I told him, and got up and walked out while he was mopping his forehead.

The typist was batting the keys at the typewriter. She didn't even look up.

Chapter Fifteen

Mrs. George Tustin Bishop surveyed me wearily.

"You again," she said.

"That's right."

There was a tired half-smile about her lips. "The bad penny."

I shook my head. "The Boy Scout. I did my good turn yesterday. I'm doing another one today."

"With me?"

"Yes."

"Purely disinterested, I suppose?" There was a touch of sarcasm in her voice.

"Wrong again."

She said, "Look, Mr. Lam, I've been up all night. I've been interrogated over and over again. I've had to view my husband's—body. My physician wanted to give me a hypodermic and put me out of circulation. I told him I'd tough it through. You can't tell what they'd do while I was asleep— But I'm tired, terribly, terribly tired."

I said, "I think I can help you. There's no harm in trying. Your husband wasn't a mining man at all."

"Don't be silly. He had half a dozen mining corporations, all kinds of claims and locations, and—"

"And," I said, "he used them as a mask so that he could report his income without telling where the income came from."

"Where did it come from, then?"

"A place in San Francisco they call The Green Door."

"What's that?"

"A gambling place."

"Sit down," she invited.

I sat down.

She took a seat opposite me.

I said, "Hartley L. Channing is planning on taking over."

"He's always seemed very nice," she said.

"Look, Irene," I told her, "you've been around. You were a strip-teaser and burlesque queen. You should know what the score is by this time."

"You've been losing a little sleep yourself, I see."

"I've been getting around."

"Who gave *you* the dirt?"

"You'd be surprised."

"Perhaps I wouldn't."

"Anyhow," I said, "we have other things to talk about. How do you stand financially?"

"My, but you move right in, don't you?"

"That's right."

"And why should I tell you how I'm fixed financially?"

"Because I'm probably the only one who's going to shoot square with you—*if* I can do myself some good by doing it—but one thing, Irene, I wouldn't double-cross you."

"No," she said musingly, "I don't think you would. What's your first name?"

"Donald."

"All right, Donald. When you stand up in front of a bunch of morons and take your clothes off four and five times a night, you get awfully damned tired of it. George came along and fell for me like a ton of bricks. At first I didn't think there was anything to it on a permanent basis, and then I realized that he really wanted to play for keeps. So I played it that way.

"His wife tried to take him to the cleaners, and I could see that he was terribly afraid of being hooked for alimony. I told him that I wanted to give him some real assurance I wasn't playing that sort of a game. I suggested a premarital agreement. He liked the idea."

"Then what?"

"Then he had his attorney draw up an agreement."

"What was in it?"

"A complete property settlement. He gave me a substantial consideration so that I—"

"How much?"

"Ten thousand dollars as my sole and separate property."

"And what did you agree in return?"

"That it covered temporary alimony, attorney's fees, permanent alimony—everything—a complete property settlement."

"But in the event of his death?"

"I don't know," she said. "I never looked it over from that viewpoint, but as I remember it he had a right to dispose of his property by will any way that he wanted."

"Did he leave a will?"

"I don't know."

"Where would it be if he left it?"

"In the hands of his attorney."

"Did he have anyone else to leave his property to?"

She shrugged her shoulders.

"Did he keep on carrying a torch after it became legal?"

"Yes, I saw to that."

"You must be clever."

"Don't make any mistake about me, Donald, I am. Perhaps not the way you think, but I know my way around.

I can take my clothes off so it brings them right up out of the chairs and packs them in the aisles. And, believe me, there's an art to it. If you don't believe it, just watch some green kid stand up and strip and then watch a real, good, artistic stripper do the same thing."

"Now," I said, "we'll get back to the first question. How are you fixed financially?"

She said, "He took out an insurance policy, and I hung on to my ten thousand dollars."

"How much of it?"

"Pretty nearly all of it."

"Your clothes and things?"

"George bought them. George encouraged me to save the ten thousand. He wanted me to have it intact as nearly as possible."

I said, "By the time the smoke clears away you'll probably find that your husband's business affairs were all tangled up in a knot, that the only thing he really had was The Green Door, that The Green Door furnished the money to pay for everything. Did you ever hear of a gambling business going through probate?"

"No."

"You probably never will."

"So what?"

I said, "Your husband was very careful to arrange things so that his personal connection with The Green Door couldn't be proven. He had his affairs in the hands of an accountant who thinks in terms of the first person singular.

"Your husband probably had some money salted away in a safety-deposit box. Perhaps Hartley Channing knows where it is. You may find a safety-deposit box full of cash and you may not, but in view of your past a lot of questions are going to be asked—a whole lot of questions—and that insurance is going to be embarrassing."

"I know," she said wearily. "That's why I don't want to go to sleep for a while. I want to get the answers to some of those questions."

I said, "You have a hillside lot here."

She nodded.

"You've been filling in a swale over there with crushed rock."

"Yes. George wanted to make a tennis court there and he wanted to use a lot of crushed rock so we'd have good drainage underneath."

"Let's go take a look at your husband's things in the garage."

"Why?"

"I think we might find a gold pan there."

"Oh, sure. George had a couple of sleeping bags and a gold pan or two, and a mortar and pestle that he used for crushing ore, and some kind of a blowtorch for testing, and things of that sort. He kept them in a closet in the garage, a sort of special locker."

"Let's go take a look."

"Why?"

"I'm just curious."

"I'm not."

I said, "I'm trying to give you a break, Irene."

"In return for what?"

"Perhaps nothing."

"Don't be silly," she said. "I've known men for a long time. They all want something. What is it you want?"

"I might be able to cut myself a piece of cake."

"Where would that leave me?"

"With the rest of the cake."

She looked me over for a minute, then said, "I suppose there's as much of an art to being a detective as there is to being a strip-tease artist; and it probably takes a little more equipment—in different places. Come on, Donald."

She led the way down the stairs into the garage and opened a door.

There was quite an assortment of junk inside.

I selected a mortar and pestle and a gold pan.

I said, "It's going to attract attention if I am seen out there with you. Take this bucket and go out to where they've been dumping the crushed rock, pick up a few samples of the crushed rock here and there. Just try to get a pretty good cross section of the type of rock that's been dumped in there. Get all the different colors you can find. If there are any tints in the rock I want to get a sample of each color."

She looked at me for a moment without saying anything, then took the pail and walked out across the yard, skirted the swimming pool, went over to the back of the lot where trucks had been driving in and dumping crushed rock, and started picking up fragments here and there.

By the time she came in I had my little workshop fixed up. I started pounding up bits of rock in the mortar, pounding with the pestle until I had them reduced to a fine powder.

"Can you tell me what the idea of this is?"

"I'm mining."

"Do you," she asked, "expect to find the crushed rock that is delivered by a gravel company filled with diamonds?"

"Not exactly," I told her. "I think we'll hit gold. I certainly hope we do. If we don't, I've put myself out on a limb."

There was a galvanized washtub over in a corner of the garage. I filled it with water, perched myself on the end of a box and went to work panning.

She leaned over my shoulder and watched me.

The surface material was quickly washed away and we got down to a deposit of black sand in the bottom of the gold pan.

That took pretty careful manipulation if I wasn't going to lose the values, and, working on that small a scale, just the difference of a color or two of gold might make a lot of difference in the value of a mine.

Then, of course, there was the chance that even if values were there they wouldn't be "free-milling." However, I thought I could tell something of what we had just by looking at the way the stuff panned out.

Gold is a beautiful metal, but no jeweler has ever been able to make gold as beautiful as when it is first seen in a gold pan nestling in a bed of black sand.

I spun the water around in the gold pan, and as the black sand washed away there was a long, wedge-shaped streamer of gold at the upper end of the little delta.

I had been expecting gold but not that much. It seemed as though the rock must have been a third black sand and a third gold.

Behind me I could hear Irene's startled exclamation.

"That's one thing about washing out gold in a gold pan. If you have ten cents' worth it looks like two million dollars' worth."

"Donald!" she exclaimed, then, after a moment, she half whispered, "Donald!"

I gave the gold pan a twist and dumped a whole bunch of gold down into the tub, washed out the pan and put it away.

"Donald, aren't you going to save that gold?"

"It would just make trouble."

I drained the water off the tailings in the tub, dumped the tailings back in the bucket, and said, "Throw those out in the yard, Irene."

She took the bucket out and dumped it, came back and

stood looking at me, with a curiously thoughtful expression on her tired face.

I said, "Take your ten thousand dollars and buy stock in the Skyhook Mining and Development Syndicate."

"But that's my husband's company."

"Sure it is. That's the last one. That's where this rock came from."

"How do you know, Donald? There are five or six companies."

"It had to come from there," I said, "because he was trying to get the bank to foreclose a loan."

"But why would he want to do that?"

"So he could write an optimistic letter to the stockholders telling them that while the company was in temporary financial trouble due to the fact that the bank was insisting on payment of a note, the stockholders should not be discouraged, that there probably were good values in the mine and they should hang on to their stock."

"Well?" she asked.

"The effect of that," I said, "would be to cause a panic on the part of the stockholders. Every one of them would want his money back. Every one that had purchased stock would be ready to throw the stuff on the market for what he could get."

"Can you tell me what this is all about?" she asked.

"Sure. People have certain habits of thought. If money is made by a mining company, people think it must come from a mine. If a check is received from a smelting company, the assumption is that it came from smelting ore out of rock.

"Your husband ran a smelting company. It paid him money in nice tinted checks. He owned mining companies that turned ore over to the smelting company.

"It never occurred to anyone that the ore was merely crushed rock and that the smelting company owned a profitable gambling house."

She studied me. "Then I should buy stock in the smelting company?"

"In the mining company, Irene. The smelting company's assets are being taken over by muscle men. Gambling houses don't go through probate."

"But how would I go about getting the stock; that is, knowing where to buy it?"

I said, "I have an idea your husband had already done some work along those lines. Let's go take a look."

We didn't have to look far. In George Bishop's desk was the rough draft of a letter to stockholders telling them not to lose faith in the company but that if they'd hang on through the period of financial adversity which ahead, they'd come out on top of the heap. The bank was bringing suit on a promissory note which had been signed to raise capital, but the mine was looking better and better and people who hung on could be almost certain of making a substantial profit, perhaps a hundred and fifty percent of their original investment, perhaps more.

It was a cleverly worded letter.

We found the list of addresses to which the letter was to be sent, together with the number of shares of stock owned by each individual.

"Want to take a chance?" I asked. "There seems to have been about thirty thousand dollars' worth of stock sold. It probably can be bought in for around fifteen or twenty thousand dollars. But you'll find that your husband kept controlling interest in the company. If you're going to inherit his property you won't have to buy anything. If not, you'd better invest this separate property of yours."

"I think I'm going to inherit," she said.

I prowled around the desk.

There were half a dozen or so heavy green cards, finely engraved with an elaborate pattern of curved lines.

They were passes to The Green Door, made out in blank, bearing the signature of Hartley L. Channing.

She looked at them in silence.

I slipped the whole bunch in my pocket. "These might come in handy," I told her.

She said nothing.

"*Do* you have an alibi for Tuesday night?" I asked her abruptly.

"Nothing— Nothing I care to use."

"Do you have a boyfriend?"

She hesitated.

"Do you?"

"Not in the way you mean. I made up my mind I'd play fair with George when I married him."

"Wasn't it rather lonely, what with him being away so much of the time?"

She looked me in the eyes. "Donald," she said, "I'm a strip-teaser; I'm an exhibitionist. Once that gets in your blood it's hard to get it out.

"I had the most supreme contempt for the *individuals* in the audiences, but the group of contemptible individuals became an entity, an audience. I loved to hear the roars of applause come up out of the darkened theater and crash against the backdrop in a wave of sound.

"I knew what they were applauding. It wasn't my acting, it was my body. They were trying to get me to take more off than the law allowed. They'd stamp and pound and applaud and go nuts."

"Didn't they know you couldn't take any more off than you had without going to jail?"

"That's just the point, Donald. They knew it but my acting was good enough so I could make them forget it. A good strip-teaser can appear to be almost undecided, as though she's just about ready to take a chance this once just to please this one particular audience. She stands there as though debating the thing within her own mind, and, of course, that spurs the audience on to the wildest applause— I tell you it's an art, standing there looking like that."

"And you miss it?"

"Donald, I miss it terribly."

"What does all that have to do with where you were Tuesday night?"

"A lot."

"Go on," I said.

She said, "I knew George was leaving. I have some friends in burlesque here, some of the old gang— Well, after George left I went up to the theater, put on a mask, and did a strip tease as the 'Masked Mystery.' I loved it— so did the management. The audience went wild. I have a perfect alibi if I dare to use it—several hundred witnesses."

"You were masked. They couldn't see your face."

"*They* couldn't, but a dozen performers knew that I was the 'Masked Mystery' and the audience knew I was there—two shows."

"Ever done that before?"

"You mean since I married George?"

"Yes."

"No. This was the first time."

I said, "It's not so good, Irene. It looks too much as if you had been manufacturing an alibi while a boyfriend did the dirty work. As an alibi it's just too darn good."

"I know," she admitted. "I'd thought of that. I wondered if you would."

"The police will," I told her. "That's the main point. What have you told the police?"

"I've told them I was home and in bed."

I said, "You've been up all night?"

"Yes."

"And haven't had much sleep for the last few days?"

"No."

I said, "Get hold of your physician. Tell him you're nervous and jumpy. Tell him you want to go to sleep and stay asleep for about twenty-four hours. If they ask you questions and you don't have the right answers, you'll be arrested."

"I know."

I said, "All right. You can't talk while you're asleep, and if when you wake up you overlook something, you can always claim it was the aftereffect of the drug that gave you hallucinations. And with your figure there isn't a juror in the world who won't give you all the breaks.

"But if you haven't been drugged, you won't sleep, and then the wrong answers will be easier to make and harder to explain.

"So give me that list of stockholders and as much money as you want to put into stock in that company, and I'll see if I can't add to your personal fortunes."

"And what will you get out of it for yourself?"

I looked her straight in the eyes. "Fifty percent of the net profit."

"Now," she said with a sigh, "I can trust you."

"Why?"

"I didn't know what you wanted before," she said, "and I get terribly distrustful of men until I know what they want."

Chapter Sixteen

The San Francisco papers put out extras when John Carver Billings and his son were arrested.

One of the papers even went so far as to spread red ink above the banner: *Banker Arrested for Bishop Murder.*

The evidence that police had unearthed was circumstantial and deadly.

Police felt certain that Bishop had not been killed on the yacht where his body had been discovered.

A fingerprint expert had found prints on one of the brass fixtures. The prints were those of bloody fingers and they were the prints of three of John Carver Billings's fingers on his right hand.

The padlock on the boat had been smashed and a new padlock had been placed on the boat. Police made a routine search of every hardware store in the neighborhood and found a storekeeper who remembered selling the padlock on Wednesday afternoon. Police showed him a photograph of John Carver Billings and the storekeeper made what the police described as an "instantaneous and positive identification."

Police divers recovered a .38 revolver at the bottom of the bay, directly beneath the banker's yacht. The numbers on the revolver showed that it had been sold to John Carver Billings for "protection" under a police permit. Ballistics experts proved that the bullet which was found in the body of George Tustin Bishop had been fired from this gun.

One bullet had gone entirely through the body and that bullet had been found by police embedded in a hole in a corner of the main cabin of the Billings yacht, the *Billingboy*. Police took up the carpet in the main cabin and found traces of bloodstains on the floor, despite the fact that every effort had been made to remove the bloodstains. Chemicals, however, used by the police disclosed definite bloodstains on the floor of that cabin.

The carpet which had been laid in the main cabin was new carpet, and that carpet had been bought by John Carver Billings on Thursday morning. Finally, making a search of the garage of the rich banker, police uncovered the original carpet which had been on the floor in the main cabin. It was bloodstained and there were hairs on the carpet. Microscopic examination showed that those hairs were identical in color, diameter, texture, and appearance with hairs from the head of George Tustin Bishop. A police expert swore positively they were Bishop's hairs.

Police as yet had been unable to find a motive for the murder, but it was known there had been a sharp difference of opinion between Bishop and the banker over financial affairs in connection with the operation of a mining company which had borrowed money at Billings's bank.

When questioned, both Billings and his son had offered alibis and the police had broken down both alibis. That of the junior Billings had been laboriously built up at considerable expense. The older Billings had stated he had been in conference with one of the bank's directors, a Waldo W. Jefferson, on Tuesday night, when the murder had apparently taken place. However, Jefferson, under police grilling, finally broke down and admitted that John Carver Billings had asked him as a personal favor to swear that they had been in conference Tuesday evening in order to provide him with an alibi in case it should be needed.

Billings had explained to Jefferson that there were certain private reasons why he had to have an alibi for Tuesday night, and Jefferson had such implicit confidence in the integrity of the bank president that he thought only some marital private affair was involved. He had therefore agreed to furnish the alibi. Murder had been a different proposition, and he had speedily weakened when confronted by police with the evidence they had gathered.

I went down to the yacht club.

There must have been fully three hundred morbid spectators milling around, peering through the meshed screen fences, walking aimlessly around on the outside, looking at the yachts from different angles.

Police cars came and went. Technical men were doing stuff aboard the yachts, searching for fingerprints, dusting with various powders.

Every once in a while some amateur photographer would try to crash the gates and an important-looking guard would ask for his pass. If the fellow didn't have any, the guard would nod to a police officer who then came up and chased the guy away fast.

I stood around for an hour or two until I felt I was developing falling arches. Finally, when one of the officers relieved the club watchman and he went to get a cup of coffee, I fell into step beside him.

"I'd like some information," I said, "and I'm a man who doesn't want something for nothing."

He flashed me an appraising sidelong glance. "The police told me to give out no information."

"Oh, this isn't about the murder," I said, laughing. "I wouldn't ask you about that. This is something else."

"What?"

"I'm trying to find out something about one of the boats."

"Which one?"

"Now there," I told him, "you have the reason I'm coming to you. I don't know which boat it was except that it had the insignia of this yacht club on it, and it was out cruising last Tuesday afternoon, a week ago. Now, my guess is that there aren't many yachts go out for a cruise in the afternoon in the middle of the week."

"You'd guess wrong," he said grinning. "On Wednesday afternoon there are lots of them."

"How about Monday?"

"Hardly any."

"Tuesday?"

"Oh, a few."

I said, "Do you keep any records of the yachts that go out?"

"No, we don't."

"You do, however, keep a record of the men who go through the gates?"

"That's right."

"Then by checking on the men who went through the gates last Tuesday afternoon, you could probably tell me something about what yachts were out?"

"The police have taken those records. They've taken the whole book as evidence. I've had to start another book."

"That's too bad."

"It doesn't make any difference except I don't have any records I can refer to."

"Tuesday afternoon," I said, and took twenty dollars from my pocket.

"I'd like the twenty," he said, "but I can't help you."

"Why?"

"My books are gone—the law took 'em."

"What's your name?"

"Danby."

"Perhaps you could make some dough anyway."

"How?"

"What time do you get off today?"

"Six at night."

"I could meet you and you could take a ride with me, sit in my car, and point out someone to me."

"Who?"

"A man you know. I don't know his name. I want to find out who he is. I'd give you twenty now. There'd be more later."

Danby gave the matter thoughtful consideration.

"In the meantime," I said, "I'd like to know a few things about your duties."

"What?"

"You can't be on duty every minute of the time," I said. "There are times when you have your back turned. There are times when you're out of the place, when you—"

"Look," he interrupted. "You talk just like the cops. There ain't no one going to get aboard one of those yachts without the man at the gate knowing it. If we leave that little cabin, even for thirty seconds, we throw a barrier gate inside of the first one and pull a switch which makes a bell ring on every float whenever someone steps on the platform. The members absolutely insist that no one except a member in good standing is permitted on the mooring. The club had a lot of trouble in a divorce case. The wife wanted to get some evidence. That was a couple of years ago. Detectives sneaked in and raided a yacht. It was quite a scandal. Since then the members have fixed things so no one who ain't a member can get into that yacht club, no one, no time."

"Doesn't it inconvenience the members sometimes when you're not there and—"

"I'm pretty nearly always right there. That's my business to be there. If anything happens and I have to go away, I throw that barrier gate down into place and it's locked. Whenever a member comes and sees that barrier gate locked he knows I'm out somewhere on the float. He also knows that the minute he pushes a foot down on that platform he rings a bell that'll tell me he's there. He knows I'm not going to keep him waiting, so he just steps into my little cabin. I don't think any of them have ever had to wait more than two minutes. I'm right up there on the job. That's my business. That's what I'm paid for."

I handed him the twenty dollars. "I'll be waiting at six o'clock tonight, Danby. Just step right into my car."

He looked at both sides of the twenty-dollar bill as though afraid it might be a counterfeit, then stalked into the restaurant without a word of thanks.

I went up and saw my broker.

"How you coming with the mining stock?" I asked.

"I'm buying it—scads of it, cheap. Lam, I wish you wouldn't do that."

"Why?"

"The stuff's no good. It's a mail-order promotion in the first place. In the second place the mine has been losing money on every carload of ore mined. In the third place it's indebted to the bank on a big loan. In the fourth place the mainspring of the whole thing was this guy, Bishop, and he's kicked the bucket.

"If you were trying to find the worst investment on earth you couldn't have picked a more likely prospect."

I grinned.

"That tells me all I want to know," he said. "Would it be all right if I picked up a few shares for my personal account?"

"Don't put the price up," I warned.

"Hell's bells, Lam, you couldn't put in enough money to jack up the price of that stock if you used a steam shovel."

"You getting a lot?"

"Lots of it."

"Keep getting the stuff," I said, and walked out.

At the appointed time I went to pick up Danby.

He wasn't too glad to see me.

"The cops may not like this at all," he said.

"The cops aren't paying you money."

"Cops have a way of getting mean when they don't like things."

I said, "Here's fifty dollars. How much unpleasantness would that account for?"

His eyes were greedy and shrewd. "All but ten dollars' worth," he said.

I added another ten, and he slowly pocketed the money.

"What do you want to do?"

I said, "We're going places."

"What sort of places?"

"Where we can sit in an automobile."

"And then what do we do?"

"If you see anyone you know you tell me."

"That's all?"

"That's all."

We drove rapidly out Van Ness Avenue, crossed Market Street, took the road to Daly City, and I slowed down as we came to the address of The Green Door.

It was an interesting enough place, pretty well disguised, all things considered.

Years ago San Francisco went in for a certain type of flat—a series of storerooms for little businesses on the ground floor, then two stories of flats above it, all with conventional bow windows and a type of architecture which is so typically San Franciscan that it can be recognized anywhere.

The Green Door was in one of these buildings.

On one side was a neighborhood grocery, a place with a small stock, that had a few neighborhood clients and carried charge accounts. The credit feature was the only way such a one-man business could compete with the big cash-and-carry markets where buying is on a mass basis, selling is for spot cash, and there is no trouble with bookkeeping, deadbeats, or failures.

On the other side was a dry-cleaning establishment. In between the two was The Green Door, a plain, unpretentious place which had its door painted a distinctive shade of green.

I cruised around and looked the place over.

Apparently patrons had been requested to park their cars half a block away. Taxicabs could pull up in front of the door, but three big, high-powered automobile jobs I saw scattered around the neighborhood were parked in unostentatious places. The street in front of The Green Door and on the other side had a few broken-down automobiles quite evidently belonging to the tenants who lived in the district.

The two stories of flats above The Green Door were just like any other flats in the neighborhood. One of them had a *For Rent* sign in the window, but the name of the real estate agency on that sign had been defunct for ten years. The others had various types of lace curtains, window shades, some of them with flowers in the window, but all giving the general outward impression of flats that were tenanted by people with different individualities and temperaments, having in common a low income and a desire for cheap rents.

This appearance, of course, was only a stage setting, a false front which was presented to the street. It was an artistic job.

Usually places running with police protection don't have to bother about an elaborate camouflage, just something that will be a sop to the public, a camouflage for the payoff which permits it to operate—just enough to keep the amateur detective from being able to spot the place in case he happens to live in the neighborhood.

In the case of The Green Door it looked as though a pretty clever attempt had been made at covering up, which might or might not indicate an absence of police protection.

The stores on each side of The Green Door were, of course, places that enjoyed a remarkably low rental. It therefore stood to reason that the managers had been given to understand that the one great virtue which a small businessman could hope to attain was to learn to mind his own damn business.

We parked the car where we could see The Green

Door and settled down to wait.

It was a long wait.

Danby asked questions at first. I let him think that the person I wanted to case would be coming to the grocery store.

Fog came drifting in over the hills. The white streamers were pushed along by a smart sea breeze. I felt the peculiar tang of fresh stimulation which is so characteristic of San Francisco air, particularly when the fog comes rolling in.

A taxicab pulled up in front of The Green Door; two men got out, pushed the door open, and went in.

There seemed to be no guard of any sort and the door apparently was kept unlocked.

"Know either one of them?" I asked Danby.

"Never saw them before, neither one of them. They didn't go to the grocery store. They went up in the apartments."

"So they did," I agreed.

We waited.

An expensive car containing a man and a woman swung around the corner, found a parking-place, and the man and woman came strolling back.

I left Danby sitting there, walked down to a hot-dog stand at the corner, and got a couple of sandwiches.

Danby was getting impatient.

"How long is this apt to last?" he inquired.

"Until midnight."

"Now wait a minute! I hadn't bargained for anything like that."

I said, "You did plenty of bargaining."

"I know, but I hadn't thought it was going to be like this."

"What *did* you think you'd be doing?"

"Well, I thought I'd have a chance to walk around and—"

"Get out and walk," I invited.

He didn't like the idea of that, either.

"You mean keep walking up and down the street until midnight?"

"If that's what you want."

"I'll sit right here."

We didn't say anything more for a while. Another taxi drove up; then a group of four men, who had evidently left their car parked on another street, came walking casually along, one of them looked rather sharply inside the car at the two of us sitting there; then they crossed over the street to The Green Door.

I didn't like that. Whoever was operating The Green Door had probably spotted us by this time and sent a delegation to look us over.

I looked over at Danby and wondered what he'd say if he realized that his fee might also include compensation for a damned good working-over.

He was a grouchy guy who had taken my money and then wished he hadn't assumed any obligation.

"This is going to be bad," he said. "If the club finds out, I'll have a hard time explaining—"

"So what?" I asked. "Where is the club going to find someone else who has your experience, someone else who knows all of the people and all of the ropes? And what if it does? When it finds out what he wants in the line of wages it'll get a terrific jolt. I'll bet it doesn't know how wages have gone up. It's probably keeping you on at the same old wages."

"No, the club has given me a couple of raises."

"How much?"

"One fifteen percent and one ten percent."

"Over how long a time?"

"Five years."

I made my laugh mirthless and sarcastic. Danby began

to meditate on whether he was underpaid and abused. I saw he liked the thought. I liked it, too. It kept his mind occupied.

I looked at my wrist watch. It was nine-fifteen.

A car drove up and parked. It was a club coupe, about three years old, but a good make and it looked well cared for. The man, who didn't seem to give a damn whether he left the car parked right in front of The Green Door or not, jumped out and looked up and down the street, then entered through the green door.

Danby said, "That's Horace B. Catlin. If he sees me here he—"

"You drive a car?" I interrupted.

"Sure."

"This fellow is a member of the yacht club?"

"That's right."

I said, "Wait here for an hour. If I'm not back inside of an hour, drive the car to this address, ask for the man in charge, and tell him the entire story of what we've been doing this evening."

He took the card which had the address and looked at it curiously.

"Let's see," he said, "that's down there. Let me see— I'm trying to get the cross street."

"Don't worry about it," I told him. "Put the card in your pocket. Be sure to ask for the man who's in charge and then tell him the story. It's a quarter past nine. If I'm not out of here by ten-fifteen go tell your story."

I slid out of the car, tossed my hat over on the seat, walked bareheaded across the street, and, just before I got to the entrance to The Green Door, looked over my shoulder.

Danby was sitting there studying the card.

I hoped he wouldn't realize that the address was that of police headquarters until he got there.

I turned the knob and pushed the green door open.

It swung back on well-oiled hinges and I stepped into a little hallway. A flight of worn board stairs, uncarpeted, echoing and splintered, stretched up to another door.

I started to raise my hand to knock on the door, then realized it wasn't necessary. I'd gone through a beam of invisible light and a little shutter slid open in the door. A pair of eyes regarded me through a small window of plate glass which must have been an inch thick.

"Got a card?" a voice asked, which evidently came through a microphone and wires.

I produced one of the cards I had picked up at Bishop's place. I had written my name in the blank line.

The eyes on the other side of the plate glass regarded the card, the voice through the loud-speaker said impatiently, "Well, shove it through the crack."

It was then I noticed for the first time the very narrow slit in the thick door.

I pushed the card into the narrow opening.

There was a period of complete silence, then I heard an electric mechanism pulling bolts back. The heavy door rumbled to one side, running on rollers on a steel rail. The heavy rumbling and the vibration of the stairs as the door moved showed the reason for the microphone and the amplification of the voice. That door must have been as heavy as the door of a vault. Looking curiously around me, I suddenly realized that the stairs were the only bits of wood in the entire entranceway. I had gone through the green door and entered a steel inspection room. A raiding party of police equipped with picks and sledge hammers couldn't have done more than dent the defenses.

"Well," the voice said impatiently, "go on in."

I noticed that the voice had said "go in" instead of "come in," so I wasn't too surprised to find on entering that the guard was no longer standing by the door. He had stepped into a steel, bulletproof closet on one side of the door. I could see the closet, but I couldn't see him. He probably had a revolver covering me.

I walked over the sunken steel rail on which the door had slid, and entered a completely new world. My feet were in a soft, thick carpet which felt like moss in a forest. The hallway glowed with the soft effect of indirect lighting. There was that atmosphere of casual, easy wealth, which is so necessary to a high-class gambling place. It's designed to put the customer on the defensive right at the start, to make him feel that he's associating with wealth and standing.

There's enough of the social climber in most people so that they fall for this stuff and consider it a privilege to be admitted to a place that specializes in taking their money. They'd walk out the worse for wear financially, but still with a certain deferential restraint. It's an atmosphere that cuts down on beefs and scenes, and makes even the thought of rigged wheels and marked cards seem a social sacrilege.

That atmosphere is a business investment and doesn't cost as much as one would think. It takes a few props. One is the paintings in heavy frames, carefully illuminated by shaded frame lamps. If the customer doesn't appreciate them he shamefacedly considers it's due to his own artistic ignorance. Actually the paintings are twenty-dollar copies in fifty-dollar frames, illuminated by ten-dollar lights.

The customer who can appreciate the price of the frame better than the worth of the painting, thinks they must be old masters. Otherwise why all the frame and illumination on the painting?

The other props are even more simple— Carpets with rich colors and sponge rubber underneath, and the artistic use of color in the draperies. In the soft, indirect lighting it looks like a million dollars. By daylight it would stink.

I entered rooms containing exactly what I had expected to find.

The first room was nothing but a conventional cocktail lounge. It had tables, cushioned stools, a bar, love seats, dim lighting, and the all but inaudible strains of organ music.

Two or three couples were at the tables. A party of three stags were at the far end of the bar with money scattered in front of them, two bottles of champagne, and all of the external evidence of celebrating a huge financial success.

I wondered whether they were also part of the props.

A coldly courteous individual handed me the card which I had left with the doorman downstairs.

"May I ask exactly what it was you were looking for, Mr. Lam?"

"Exactly what you have here," I said.

The cold eyes softened a bit. "May I ask where you got your card? Who vouched for you when you got it?"

I said, "The card's properly signed."

"I know, but sometimes signed cards are given to various sources for distribution."

I said, "This was given me by the owner."

He looked a little surprised then, turned it over, and said, "You know Mr. Channing personally then?"

"That's right."

"Then the situation is entirely different," he said. "Just go right on in, Mr. Lam."

Before I could move, and as though he had been struck with an afterthought, he said apologetically, "I am afraid I'm going to have to comply with the regulations and ask to look at your driving license and make sure you're the person described on the card."

"Oh, sure," I said, and flipped open my wallet, showing him my driving license.

"From Los Angeles, eh?"

"That's right."

"That's probably why I don't place you. You're going to be up here for a while, Mr. Lam?"

"Not long. I want a little action while I'm here. I am familiar with Al's place down in Los Angeles."

"Oh," he said. "How *is* Al?"

"I don't know him personally," I said, "just the place. I know the manager there—"

I stopped abruptly as though I had caught myself just in time to keep from using a name.

"Well?" he asked.

I smiled. "If you know the man I mean, you know his name. If you don't know the man I mean, there's no point in mentioning his name."

He laughed. "Did you wish to make any arrangements for credit, for having checks cashed, or anything, Mr. Lam?"

"I think I have enough cash to see me through."

"If you'd like to make any credit arrangements—"

"I'll do that when I run out of cash. I'll run in and see Channing personally in case that happens."

"Go on in, Mr. Lam."

He indicated a door at the far end of the room, around the end of the bar.

I walked around the bar, pushed open the door, and once more found myself in a hallway. At one end was a door marked *His* and at the other end a door marked *Hers*. An attendant stood in the hallway.

A buzzer made sounds. Three quick distinct buzzes.

The white-coated attendant, without a word, pulled on a lever and a concealed door slid back.

I entered the gambling rooms. There wasn't much of a crowd at the moment. Probably the heavy spenders would come later, after the dinner and theater hours.

Here again the atmosphere of synthetic luxury was carried out. There were the usual roulette and crap tables, a couple of twenty-one games, and a poker game.

From the fact that some six or eight of the persons present at the tables were dressed for the evening and were wagering rather large stakes with that impeccable hauteur which is the sucker's idea of the well-bred, upper class gambler, I knew they were the stooges who are employed to keep the place from seeming too lonely during the early evening, and to encourage play during the later hours.

Horace B. Catlin wasn't among those present.

If there had been anything depressing to the club about the news of George Tustin Bishop's death, there was no outward indication. Play went on with the smooth decorum of an exclusive club where men were gentlemen and the loss of a few hundred dollars was merely one of life's amusing incidents to be dismissed with a well-bred shrug of the shoulders.

Later on, when the play became more spirited, some of the stooges would lose large sums with a patronizing smile, then begin to rake in great sacks of chips with a sophisticated lift of the eyebrow to indicate a complete control of the emotions.

The suckers who didn't stand a chance of winning a dime would be tempted to ape their "well-bred" neighbors at the table, and they, too, would shrug off their losses with a patronizing smile, wait in vain for "luck" to turn, and then go outside really to beef.

There are, of course, a few square gambling houses in the United States. Somehow I had the impression The Green Door wasn't one of those few.

I watched for a while, then went over and bought a twenty-dollar stack of chips. The man who presided over the wheel flashed a diamond as his well-manicured, skillful fingers slid the chips out to me in a careless gesture. His entire attitude seemed to say that the place was broad-minded, and if a piker wanted to get a stack of chips for twenty dollars, it was quite all right with the management. They were running a democratic house.

I bet five dollars on red and the wheel came black. I doubled my bet on red. Red came up and paid off. I put two dollars on number three and number thirty came up. I put another two dollars on number three and number seven came up.

Again I put two dollars on number three and number three came up. The man in charge of the game paid off and honored me with a quizzical glance. Some of the other people began to size me up.

I left two dollars on the three and played two dollars on the twenty.

The twenty came up, and the man in charge once more slid out a stack of chips.

He also paused to adjust his tie.

I put two dollars on the five.

There was a nervous feminine laugh. I saw the flash of bare shoulder as an arm reached across so that the flesh all but brushed my cheek. A young vision said, "I hope you don't think I'm forward, but with luck like yours I'm not going to pass up a chance to ride along."

"Not at all," I said politely, and looked her over.

She was blond, with a cute, upturned nose, a rosebud mouth, and a figure which could well have won prizes in any bathing-beauty parade.

She smiled up at me with just the right amount of cordiality and then almost instantly became somewhat coldly aloof, as though suddenly realizing that, after all, she didn't know who I was and our acquaintanceship had stemmed from the fact that we happened to be standing at a roulette table together.

The wheel spun, the ball clattered, and number seven came up.

I put two dollars on number ten. The blonde put two dollars right on top of mine.

The wheel spun and we lost.

I put two dollars on number twenty-seven. The blonde hesitated a moment, then put a dollar bet on the top of mine.

The wheel spun, the ball clattered, and number twelve came.

I heard the blonde sigh. I put two dollars on number seven and a dollar on number three.

The blonde hesitated, then, as though trying bravely to conceal the fact that this was her last dollar, she put a chip on number three, right on top of mine.

The ball spun around and popped into a pocket. The blonde saw it before I did. She gave a startled squeal and grabbed my arm in an ecstasy of enthusiasm that she couldn't quite control.

"We've done it!" she cried. "We've done it! We've won!"

The man at the wheel gave her a fatherly glance of dignified, quiet amusement and paid us off.

We bet together three or four times more, then we won again.

I was beginning to get a fair-sized pile of chips.

The blonde nervously took a cigarette case from a black bag and tapped the cigarette on the side of the polished silver. She inserted it in her mouth, and I snapped a match into flame.

She leaned forward for the light.

I could see the long curling eyelashes, the mischievous glint of saucy hazel eyes, as she looked me over with demure interest.

"Thank you," she said, and then after a moment added, "for everything."

"Don't thank me," I told her.

"Lots of people wouldn't like to have me—well, share their luck." Her glance was of the type to inspire a man to say that it would be a pleasure to share everything he had with her on a permanent basis.

I merely smiled.

Her hand rested on mine for an instant as she moved her pile of chips an inch or two along the side of the table.

Abruptly she said, "It means so much, so very, very much to me, and I was down to my last dollar."

We lost three or four more bets, then I put five dollars on a number. She suddenly felt lucky and put ten dollars above my five.

The number paid off.

Her scream of delight was almost instantly suppressed as though she was afraid she might be put out, but she looked up at me and her eyes were dancing. Once more her hand was on my arm, the fingers digging in through the coat. "Oh," she said, and then after a moment, "Oh!"

The man at the wheel paid off my bet, seemed to frown with annoyance as he paid off the blonde's bet. It was a sizable bunch of chips.

She leaned against me. I could feel her tremble.

"I've got to go where I can sit down," she said. "Please— Please, what can I do about my—about my chips?"

"Cash them in, if you wish," the dealer said carelessly, "and then you can buy in again when you get ready to play."

"Oh, I— Very well."

Her weight was heavy against me as though her knees were getting ready to buckle.

"Please," she said in a half-whisper, "can you help me over to a chair?"

I gave a quick glance at my stack of chips and at hers.

The man at the wheel caught my eye and nodded. "I'll take care of it," he said, with the gesture of one who disdains to consider money of any great importance.

I took the girl's arm and helped her out to a table at the bar.

A waiter hovered over us solicitously as soon as we were seated.

"The occasion," I said, "would seem to call for celebration. Would you care for champagne?"

"Oh, I'd love it. I have to have—something. Oh, it means so much! Would you— Could you—"

"Certainly," I said, "if you wish. I'll see about getting your money for you. Do you know how much you had coming?"

She shook her head.

"Under those circumstances, I'm afraid you'd better attend to the financial transaction yourself."

"Oh, it's quite all right. I know you're on the up-and-up. I—I wouldn't have had a thing if it hadn't been for you, Mr.—"

"Lam," I said.

"I'm Miss Marvin," she said, smiling. "My friends call me Diane."

"My name's Donald."

"Donald, I'm just too absolutely, completely flabbergasted to get up and walk into that room. My legs just seem to turn to water. I— Well, I just wish you could see my knees."

"It's an idea," I said.

"Oh," she said, making a little slap at me. "I didn't mean it *that* way."

One of the assistant managers bent gravely over the table. "Did you people wish to cash in your chips," he asked, "or would you prefer to have them brought to you here in the bar? You can use them to pay for anything in the house."

"Let's hang on to them," she said instantly. "Could you— Well, could they be brought out here?"

"But certainly."

He bowed, vanished, and a moment later came back with a plastic container in which my chips had been placed, and a polished wooden rack in which the girl's chips were stacked.

"We took the liberty of changing some of these chips," he said, "so they wouldn't be so bulky. The blue chips represent twenty dollars each."

"Those blue chips—twenty dollars for each one?"

"That's right."

Her fingers caressed the edges of the gold-embossed chips. "Each one," she said in an awed half-whisper, "twenty dollars."

The waiter brought champagne, popped the cork, spilled ice out of the glasses and filled them to the brim.

We touched glasses.

"Here's luck," I said.

"Here's to *you*," she countered. "You're *my* luck."

We sipped the champagne. Her eyes studied me. She said abruptly, "I'm betwixt and between."

"What do you mean?"

She said, "I need money. I have just about half enough here. I'll be frank with you. I was down to my last cent. I came up here and invested every cent I could scrape up to buy chips. I made up my mind I'd either get what I wanted or be completely broke, and then I'd—"

Her voice trailed away into a significant silence.

"Then you'd what, my dear?" I asked.

"I don't know. I hadn't gone that far. Either sell myself or kill myself, I guess."

I said nothing.

She studied me thoughtfully. "What should I do? Should I quit now, play it safe and try to raise the rest of the money some other way, or should I go ahead and gamble?"

"On those matters," I said, "I give no advice."

"You've been my inspiration, my luck. You've brought me success. Everything was going bad for me. And then you came along."

I said nothing.

Abruptly the floor manager glided up to the table. "Would you mind stepping into the office?" he asked Diane.

"Oh," she said, her knuckles suddenly white as she pressed her fist against her lips. "What have I done now?"

The manager's smile was reassuring. "Nothing," he said. "Only I have been asked to invite you to step into the office, Miss Marvin, and the boss would like to see Mr. Lam, too." '

I glanced at my watch. It was thirty-five minutes from the time I had entered the place. I still hadn't seen anything of Horace B. Catlin.

Abruptly Diane Marvin pushed back the chair. "Come on," she said. "Let's get it over with."

"What is it?" I asked.

"Probably something about my credit—about— I don't know."

The floor manager escorted us deferentially to a big door marked *Private*.

He swung the door open without touching it, apparently by putting weight on a concealed button.

"Right this way, please," he said, standing aside.

I followed Diane into an office.

The floor manager didn't come in. The door clicked shut behind us. I turned to look. There was no knob on the door.

There were comfortable chairs grouped in a half-circle around a table on which were glasses, a decanter, ice, and soda.

A plain door at the far end of the office opened and Hartley L. Channing said, "Right this way, please."

We walked in.

Channing shook hands with both of us. "How are you, Lam?" he said.

"Fine," I told him.

He didn't say anything to Diane.

She walked on into the inner office and I followed.

This was a room fixed up both as a den and an office. There were a television set, a radio, phonograph, a safe, filing cabinet, a desk, and comfortable lounging chairs. There were bookcases, paneled walls, indirect lighting, and there wasn't a window in the place. An air conditioning unit kept a stream of fresh air flowing in and out.

Channing turned to Diane and said, "You can lay off, Diane. He's not a fish."

She said indignantly, "Well, then, why the hell didn't I get the signal? I—"

"Keep your shirt on," he told her. "There's been a mix-up."

"I'll say there's been a mix-up! I had things coming along just fine and—"

"That'll do," he told her. "You can go now. Forget you've seen this man, that you've been here, forget everything."

Without a word to me she got up and flounced out through the door.

I couldn't tell whether she had the combinations so that she knew how to open the door which had no knob, or whether there was some secret connection at Channing's desk by which he could open it.

Channing and I looked at each other across the desk.

"I'd like to see the card by which you got past the doorman, Lam."

I smiled at him.

"Well?" he said, extending his hand. "I'm waiting."

I said, "The card was good enough to get me in. Isn't that good enough for you?"

"No."

I made no move.

Channing frowned. "You certainly aren't naïve enough to think I don't control the situation here," he said.

I said, "I certainly hope you aren't naïve enough to think I'd let you know *what* I'm thinking."

"This isn't getting us anywhere."

"It's got me this far."

"That may not prove to be entirely beneficial—for you."

I stole a glance at my wrist watch. I had a little over nineteen minutes to go.

I said, "Perhaps you and I might talk without chasing each other around in circles, and really get somewhere."

"I want to see that card."

I said nothing.

I didn't see Channing give the signal—probably a concealed button somewhere under the desk—but abruptly the door from the outer office opened and a man in a tuxedo stood quietly on the threshold.

"Mr. Lam," Channing said, "had a card when he entered the place."

The newcomer said nothing.

"He doesn't wish to produce that card," Channing said. "I'd like very much to look at it."

The man moved forward, smiling serenely. "The card, Mr. Lam," he said.

I made no move.

The man hesitated briefly by my chair.

Channing nodded.

The man reached forward and grabbed my wrist. I tried to jerk the arm free. I might as well have tried to pull against a steel cable.

Swift, efficient fingers did things to the wrist. The other hand hit against my elbow. My arm doubled around, flew up against my back, the wrist was doubled into a grip that pulled the tendons until it was all I could do to keep from screaming.

"The card," Channing said.

I twisted my body, trying to ease the tension and the pain as much as possible.

"Of all the damn fools," Channing said, and came over to search me.

I was powerless to make a move.

Channing's hand shot into my inside pocket, came out with my wallet. He deftly extracted the card I had used in entering the place, started to put the wallet back, then thought better of it and took the wallet and the card over to his desk.

"That's all, Bill," he said.

The man in the tuxedo released the grip on my wrist.

I dropped back into the chair. My arm felt as though every tendon in it had been pulled out of place.

Channing started to tell Bill to go, then thought better of it. "Stick around, Bill," he said.

Channing said, "Lam, I don't like this. You sat around in front for several hours with a companion. The man is still down there waiting for you. I suppose if you don't appear within a certain time he's to come and get you or else call the police. Is that it?"

"You're talking. I'm listening."

"I suppose you feel that gives you a paid-up policy of life insurance."

"I'll run my business," I said, "you run yours."

He examined the card carefully.

"This is a genuine card," he said. "It not only bears my signature but it has the little secret mark on it that you wouldn't even know was there. It's a genuine card. Where did you get it?"

"It was given to me."

He shook his head. "Those cards aren't obtained in that way."

I said nothing.

He studied the card again, then looked over at me and I didn't like what I saw in his eyes.

"Lam," he said, "I'm not going to tell you *how* I know, but this is one of the cards that were given to George Bishop for distribution to a very select few.

"Ordinarily George kept his connection with this place completely secret, but for the few people whom he knew he could trust, he had some special cards. This is one of those cards. Now where did *you* get it?"

"It was given to me."

"You know, Lam, there's just a chance, just an outside chance that you've been over talking with Irene Bishop. I wouldn't like that."

I said nothing.

He picked up my wallet, started going through it, became motionless. "Well, I'm damned," he said, half under his breath. "You've got four more cards—all given to George Bishop!"

I realized then how foolish I had been to keep this evidence on me. There undoubtedly was a secret mark on each of those cards.

For ten or fifteen seconds he sat there, saying nothing.

I stole another glance at my wrist watch. I had eleven minutes to go, then Danby would call the police *if* he followed instructions. I hoped he'd follow instructions. I didn't care particularly about having the police butt in at this stage of the game, but I could see that things might be getting just a little out of hand.

Abruptly Channing said, "Bill, there's a man waiting down there in the guy's car. I had assumed he was just an errand boy carrying a life insurance policy for this guy, but I think we'd better make sure."

"Yes?" Bill said.

"Go down and bring him in," Channing said.

"Suppose he doesn't want to come?"

"I told you to *bring him in.*"

Bill started moving for the door.

I knew I had to stall for ten and a half minutes.

"We might talk first," I said.

"We might talk afterward," Channing retorted.

I got up out of the chair, said, "I think I'm tired of being pushed around."

I hoped that would bring Bill back to pull another judo grip on me and delay things for a while.

Bill looked questioningly at Channing.

Channing said, "Get going, Bill," and pulled a .38 revolver out of the top drawer in the desk.

"I think," he said, "I'm going to readjust a lot of opinions within the next few minutes. I'm readjusting some right now. So you really are a private detective. What the hell are you working on, and who the hell are you really working for?"

The door closed behind Bill. I knew I was sunk then. I should have cut the time limit down to thirty minutes, gone in and got out.

And really I didn't want the police any more than Channing did. That probably was why I'd made it an extreme outside limit. I had really expected to go in there, get the information I wanted, and be out inside of half an hour. I'd have done it, too, if it hadn't been for Diane Marvin. The fact that the man behind the roulette wheel had given her the signal to start playing me for a live one had given me a false sense of security.

Channing thought things over for a while, then tossed the wallet across the desk so it lit in my lap.

"Put it away," he said. "I don't want you to think we'd take anything by force here. You'll find that everything's in your wallet. I just wanted to look at it—and it's a damned good thing I did."

"Okay," I said, "what do we do next?"

"We wait."

I said, "I was having a bottle of champagne with your come-on out there. I suppose the champagne is still waiting. It—"

"Don't mention it, Lam," he said magnanimously, "there'll be no charge. In fact, I'll have it brought in here. I may want to use it for a christening."

"What christening?"

"I think I'll pour it all over you and christen you the heel of the week."

"That won't get you any place."

"Shut up, I want to think."

We were silent for a while, then a loudspeaker said, "Bill is at the door. He says to tell you he has a man with him."

Channing said, "Tell him to take the guy into office number two and plug in the sound connection. Question him in there. You can help him with the questions. I want to find out who this guy is and what he's doing around here."

"I suppose," Channing said, turning to me, "you have one of your agency men with you."

I said nothing.

"You're a communicative cuss, aren't you?"

"My clients pay me to get information, not to give it."

"Who are your clients, by the way?"

I grinned at him.

"I wonder," he said softly, almost to himself, "if Irene is just a little smarter than we've been thinking she is."

I still said nothing.

"If Irene wants to make any trouble," he said, his eyes narrowing, "it would be a dirty, nasty mess—for her. She wouldn't get anything out of it. Make no mistake, Lam, I've taken over here and that's final. There isn't the scratch of a pen that ties George Bishop into this thing. There isn't anyone who can show this isn't my business built with my money, and there isn't any way of passing this thing on to George's widow. She wouldn't stand one chance in a million."

He waited for a few minutes, then said, "I wish I knew whether you were working for her or not."

Abruptly a light flashed. Channing reached over and tripped a switch. He said to me, "We can hear what goes on in the other room but they can't hear what's said in here."

Almost instantly a voice said, "All right, buddy, let's have it. What's your name?"

"My name is Danby, and I didn't want to come in here. I'm going to make charges against you. You can't hustle me around like this. That's kidnaping."

"Danby, eh? What do you do?"

"That's none of your business."

"Let's take a look for a driving license."

There was the sound of a brief scuffle and another voice said, "Okay, this is it. Frank Danby. Here's his social security number and—"

"What's the address on that driving license?"

"A yacht club."

"Good Lord, I get it now," Channing said, coming up out of the chair as though the thing had been wired.

He crossed the room, jerked the door open, and was out like a shot.

I got up and crossed over to the desk.

He'd taken the revolver with him.

I gave every drawer in the desk a quick frisking. There wasn't another gun anywhere in the place. There was a box of .38 shells, a pipe, a tobacco pouch, and a can of tobacco. There were two packages of cigarettes, a box of cigars, some chewing gum, and a bottle of fountain-pen ink.

Aside from that .38-caliber gun it was a desk that the police could have prowled through any day in the week, and welcome.

Abruptly I heard Channing's voice from the other room. "What's the trouble?"

Danby's voice, surly and defiant, said, "I've been kidnaped. Who are you?"

"Kidnaped!" Channing exclaimed.

"That's what I said. This guy made me come in here with him. He had a gun in his pocket."

Channing said, "What's all this, Bill?"

Bill's voice said, "No gun, just a lead pencil. For a gag I pushed the end of this lead pencil against the cloth of the coat pocket."

"But what was the trouble?" Channing asked.

"No trouble except this guy has been sitting out front getting a line on everyone coming in. I figured he's a stickup guy, waiting for some dough-heavy customer to come out. Then he'd follow and stick 'em up."

"That's serious," Channing said. "We'd better turn him in."

"You're nuts," Danby growled, but his voice showed he was frightened. "You've got nothing on me. I was hired to come out to point out a guy."

"Who?"

"I don't know, but when I recognized Mr. Catlin, this fellow left me and came on in."

Channing's booming laugh was good-natured. "Oh,

shucks, that must have been Donald Lam."

"That's the guy," Danby said. "His name is Lam. He told me if he didn't get out inside of an hour to call a friend."

Channing said, laughing, "That's a shame. He left a message for you and I intended to deliver it, but I had no idea it was— Why, he said you were his chauffeur."

"What did he say?"

"Lam found the man he wanted to see here and they went out the back way. He thought at first this fellow might make trouble and that's why he told you about calling the friend. But there wasn't any trouble and Lam left. Seems he's a private detective. I didn't know whether you knew. I've known Lam for ten years and he's all right, straight as a string."

"What was his trouble with Mr. Catlin?" Danby asked.

"No trouble with Catlin. Catlin was helping Lam. Catlin was to point out the guy Lam wanted. I should have notified you sooner, but I've been busy. Lam told me to tell you either to drive the car back to the yacht club, or to telephone for a taxicab, whichever you wanted to do. He left me five dollars to give you to pay for the cab. He's been gone about twenty minutes."

"Do I get the five-spot if I drive the car back to the yacht club or only if I take a taxi?" Danby asked.

I knew then I was sunk. There was no use waiting to hear any more. I started prowling, trying to find a way out.

I looked around the desk for buttons I could press that would unlatch the door. I tried to remember just what Channing had been doing before he streaked across the office.

Abruptly the door swung open. I felt certain I'd pressed the right button and was halfway across the office before I realized the door was being opened from the outside.

Bill was coming back in. Apparently Channing had given him a signal.

Bill grinned at me and said, "Sit down, Lam."

I tried to duck around past him and grab the door before it closed.

Bill snaked out an arm, caught me by the back of the coat, spun me around, clamped his fingers around my sore wrist, and said, "Right in that chair, Lam."

I hit him in the stomach with everything I had. Sheer surprise made him recoil. That and the force of the blow gave me freedom for a second. I threw myself against the door which had been slowly swinging shut.

Bill charged, but I had the door open and was out in the reception room, running across it with Bill in hot pursuit.

The door opened.

Bill yelled a warning. I flung myself into the opening just as Channing started in. I hit Channing as though he had been a line of scrimmage.

My momentum plowed him back, but I was slowed up enough for Bill's long arm to reach out. His fingers grabbed the back of my coat collar.

Something hit me on the side of the head. A wave of blackness came up from my stomach. The bitter of nausea was in my mouth and my knees went limp.

I tried to hang onto the doorknob, turning around, jerking my head back as I did so.

I had a glimpse of Bill, his arm upraised, a blackjack looped around his wrist. There was no expression on his face. He even looked slightly bored.

Then the arm chopped down.

There was a blinding flash inside my brain and the floor smacked my face.

Chapter Seventeen

I had no idea what time it was when I regained consciousness. I was sprawled on a bed in a cheap, dingy bedroom equipped with an iron bedstead, a chair, a dresser, a washstand, and a wardrobe closet.

It was the sort of cheap furniture that could have been picked up at a secondhand store, completely different from the sumptuous, synthetic elegance of the gambling house—and yet a subconscious feeling existed that I was still within the confines of the gambling house.

Bill was sitting in a chair reading one of the so-called true detective magazines. The chair was almost directly beneath a single electric light hanging from a twisted green drop cord and covered with a green shade.

I moved my head and the room started rocking around as though it were a cabin on a boat in a heavy sea.

I felt sick.

Bill turned a page in the magazine, then looked over at me as a precautionary measure, saw my eyes were open, pushed a thick forefinger in between the pages of the magazine to mark his place, put the magazine down, and grinned. "How you feelin', buddy?"

"Rotten."

"You'll feel better after a while."

He got up out of the chair, picked a bottle from the dresser, unscrewed the top, and held it under my nose.

It was a smelling salt that did a great deal to revive me.

"Now, just take it easy," Bill cautioned sympathetically. "You ain't hurt bad. Just roughed up a bit. You'll be all right."

Gradually the throbbing left my head. The room steadied down and my head settled into a dull, constant ache with a sore spot above and back of my right ear that felt like a boil.

"What's the idea?" I asked.

Bill read a couple more interesting paragraphs in the magazine before he looked up to answer the question. "I'm not supposed to talk."

"What *are* you supposed to do?"

"Keep you right here."

I said, "That could be pretty serious, you know, in case I wanted to get up and walk out."

"How come?"

"Kidnapping."

He grinned. "Save your breath, buddy."

I swung around to a sitting position on the bed.

Bill watched me with quizzical interest.

I slowly got up.

Bill put down the magazine. "Now, listen, Lam," he said, "you're a nice egg but you've got yourself poured into the wrong pan. You've led with your chin and you should be smart enough to know that that's going to make trouble."

"What's Channing planning to do?" I asked.

"I don't think he's made up his mind yet."

"He's got to let me go sometime."

The smile left Bill's face. "Don't be too sure about that. You don't know some of the things I know."

"What?"

"I told you I'm not talking. Now, shut up. I'm going to read. I won't talk, and I don't want to listen."

"You're working for Channing, aren't you?"

"That's right."

"Like your job?"

"I'm getting by all right."

"Loyalty is a fine thing," I said, "but self-preservation is the first law of nature. You'd better start thinking about yourself."

He laughed a heavy, mirthless laugh. "Look who's talking. *You're* the one who should be thinking about yourself. You should have done that before you ever came into the joint."

I said, "Do you think I'm foolish enough to have gone into this place unless I knew what I was doing?"

I saw interest in his eyes. "You were probably just taking a big chance."

I said, "Don't kid yourself. You know what's been going on in the background. Gabby Garvanza wanted to muscle in on the situation up here. Gabby Garvanza got put on the spot and stopped a lot of lead. The trouble was the fellow who did the job was a little nervous and the bullets weren't put in the right places to do the job.

"Now Gabby Garvanza's well and he's up here in San Francisco. What do *you* suppose he came up here for?"

Bill closed the magazine.

I said, "The real owner of this joint was George Tustin Bishop. Channing was simply the front who handled the accounts and juggled the figures around.

"Maurine Auburn had been Bishop's girlfriend. He threw her over when he divorced his wife and married Irene, the strip-tease artist. Bishop was getting rid of both his wife and his mistress at the same time. That's how wrapped up he was in Irene. Maurine took up with Gabby Garvanza, but she'd always carried a torch for George Bishop.

"Maurine was supposed to be Gabby Garvanza's girl. Someone tried to rub Gabby out. Maurine saw the whole thing. She wasn't hurt. No bullets were fired in her direction. She didn't say anything. Why?"

I could see Bill was thinking.

"The reason," I said, "could have been because the

gunman was someone she liked very much. That someone liked her so well he wouldn't want her hurt. He knew she liked him enough so that he knew he could depend on her not to squeal.

"Then Gabby began to get well, and Gabby knew who had shot him. Gabby started planning to go to San Francisco and even scores.

"Maurine wanted to warn her friend. She wanted to make certain that the next attempt on Gabby's life was going to hit the jackpot. You think back on that story the newspaper tells about how she walked out on the people who were with her—bodyguards that had been provided by Gabby to see that nothing happened to her.

"She pretended to get crocked, to pick up with some fellow whom she met by chance— Well, I did a little checking of my own. That fellow was an aviator. Maurine picked him up, all right, but they didn't go out making whoopee together. They dashed out to the airport. The fellow she'd picked up cranked up his plane and made a blue streak to a field up north of San Francisco, where the plane let down and Maurine and George Bishop were scheduled to have a secret confab and lay plans so Gabby Garvanza would cuddle up on a nice cold slab in the morgue.

"Somebody was there waiting. Someone who felt that a lot of good could be accomplished by getting George Bishop out of the picture in such a manner that he would seem to have a perfect alibi."

"Gabby Garvanza?" Bill asked.

I snorted derisively. "Gabby wouldn't have gone to all that trouble. Who was it who profited the most by Bishop's death?"

Bill thought that over, then stirred restlessly. "I don't like the chin music you're making," he said. "Even listening to it could get me into trouble."

"*Not* listening to it could get you into a hell of a lot more trouble. How big a damn fool do you think Gabby is? Gabby Garvanza is in San Francisco right this minute. Hartley Channing pulled a pretty slick deal but he committed a murder."

"John Billings killed Bishop," Bill said.

I smiled and shook my head. "Bishop's body was put aboard Billings's yacht. That was done by someone who knew that once the body was found there people wouldn't look any farther for the real criminal than young Billings. Billings thought he was smart. He sneaked the body over onto an adjoining yacht. What he didn't realize was that Bishop had been killed with his gun and that the murderer had dropped the gun overboard from the stern of Billings's yacht. It never occurred to Billings to think of that or to go down in the drink and take a look. But that was the first thought that occurred to the police. That's why the diver working with an underwater metal locator found the gun in the first fifteen minutes. Gabby Garvanza knows these things. *Now* what do you think he's going to do?"

"How do you know Gabby Garvanza knows them?"

I grinned at him and said, "Who the hell do you think hired *me?*"

Bill sat up straight in the chair. He studied me thoughtfully for a few moments, then gave a low whistle.

He tossed the magazine over onto a battered table and said, "What do you want, Lam? If I let you get away from me Channing would kill me before Gabby ever took over."

I said, "Let me get to a phone."

"That would be too hard."

I said, "Lots of things are going to be hard. Don't think for a minute Gabby Garvanza doesn't know what's going on here. You rub me out and the chances that you'll live to see your next birthday are just about a million to one—and

I don't give a damn if your next birthday is the day after tomorrow."

Bill's forehead knitted into a frown.

I said, "The police will find the aviator who took Maurine up here within—"

"Shut up," he blurted. "I want to think. If you're as smart as I think you are, you'll keep your damned trap closed for the next five minutes."

I eased back on the bed. The pillow propped under my neck took some of the soreness out of the aching head.

It wasn't five minutes, not much over two minutes, when Bill said, "There's a phone booth down at the end of the hall. Now, for the love of Mike don't make any noise and don't let anybody see you."

I got up off the bed. Bill took my arm to steady me.

"Got any money?" Bill asked.

I ran my hand clown into my trousers pocket and encountered the small change. "Okay," I said.

"Okay," Bill told me. "You're on your own. If anyone spots you I'm going to put a slug in your ribs and claim you were escaping."

He opened the door, looked up and down the corridor, then nodded to me.

I eased my way down the hall and into the phone booth, closed the door, and tried to recall the number of Gabby's hotel. The thought of having to look it up in the phone book was an agony to my aching eyes and I couldn't take any chances with the delay.

I remembered the number, dropped a coin, and spun the dial on the telephone.

When the hotel answered I said, "George Granby, please."

I could hear the connection being made. Realizing how much depended on Gabby being in and talking with me, I could feel my hand begin to shake and my knees quiver at the mere thought that he might not be there.

The man who answered the telephone was undoubtedly the bodyguard who had thrown me out.

"Put Gabby on," I said.

"Who is this?"

"This," I told him, "is Santa Claus and it's Christmas. Get Gabby on fast or his stocking will be empty."

I heard the guy say, "Some nut says he's Santa Claus passing out information. You want to talk with the goof?"

I heard Gabby rumble something, and then the bodyguard said, "Go peddle your papers."

I said, "This is Donald Lam, the private detective, whom you threw out a while back."

"Oh-oh," the man said.

I said, "I've completed my investigations up here. I told Gabby I might do him a good turn. Now I'm in a position to do it."

"What way?"

"By giving him information about what I've uncovered."

"We don't give a damn what you found out. We know what we want to know."

"You think you do," I said. "You'd better know what I know and then you'll know who killed Maurine Auburn and why. Ask Gabby if he's interested."

This time I couldn't hear anything. The bodyguard was evidently holding his palm over the transmitter so I couldn't, but after what seemed an interminable wait, and after Central had asked, "Are you waiting?" Gabby Garvanza's voice said cautiously, "Start talking. Give me facts. To hell with what you think. Give me facts."

"I told you I might be able to do you some good," I said. "Now I'm—"

"Can the chatter. Give me facts."

I said, "You've known Maurine for over a year. How many times in that year has she got drunk enough to start playing around with strangers? The business of getting boiled and walking out on the bodyguard was part of an act. The fellow she went out with was an aviator. He took her to San Francisco."

"Any damn fool could put two and two together on that," he said, "now that her body's been found."

I said, "All right, she went of her own accord, under her own power, on an errand she didn't dare to tell you about and didn't dare to let the bodyguard know about. The errand was that she wanted to keep a rendezvous with George Bishop."

"That all?" Gabby asked.

"George Bishop shot you," I said.

Silence at the other end of the line.

"Maurine put the finger on you."

"You talk a lot," Gabby said.

"You wanted facts. There they are."

"You got proof—about Maurine?"

"Of course."

"Well," Gabby rasped, "spill it."

I said, "The man who killed both Bishop and Maurine was Hartley L. Channing. He wants to take over The Green Door. He knew that with Bishop out of the way and enough murder mixed up in the thing the police wouldn't dare let you muscle in up here."

"Where are you now?"

"Right now," I said, "I'm being held prisoner by Channing. I think he intends to pour some nice wet concrete around me and clunk me in the deepest part of San Francisco Bay. I'd like like hell to have you do something about it before—"

"How did you get to the phone?"

I said, "I talked my guard into the idea that you were

going to be the new boss."

Once more there were four or five seconds of silence, then he said, "You're a naïve son of a bitch."

"I'm talking, ain't I?"

"Sure, you're talking," he said, "and your guard was Bill. Right?"

I hesitated a moment, and in that moment realized why it had been so easy to sell Bill on letting me talk to Gabby.

"Right," I said.

"All right," he said, "let me talk to Bill."

I left the receiver dangling and tiptoed back to the room.

"Your boss wants you on the line," I told Bill.

Without a word he got up and walked out, leaving me sitting there on the bed.

I wanted to give it an artistic touch. I went over and picked up Bill's magazine. When he came back I was deeply engrossed in reading one of the so-called true detective cases.

"Come on," he said, "you're going out."

I slowly got up from the bed.

He looked at me curiously.

"How the hell did you know I was one of Gabby's men?" he asked.

I didn't answer that question. I'd made the only play I had to make and the fact that Lady Luck had dumped the jackpot into my lap was just her way of squaring up for the bum break she'd given me when Frank Danby spilled his guts to Hartley Channing and sold me down the river.

I tried to look modest.

"You might be a smart bastard," Bill said. "Come on, let's go."

Chapter Eighteen

From my cheap hotel I called police headquarters and got Lieutenant Sheldon on the line.

"Donald Lam speaking," I said.

"Son of a gun," Sheldon said. "Where are you, Donald?"

I gave him the address of the hotel.

"What are you doing there?"

"I've been hiding out."

"What from?"

"Oh, I didn't want to break in on your time. I knew you were a busy man and I thought some of your boys were trying to take me up to see you."

"You shouldn't have been so considerate, Donald. I *want* to see you. I want to see you pretty damn bad. In fact, I've had the word out to pick you up wherever you happen to be, either here or when you showed up in your office at Los Angeles."

"I'll be glad to see you, Lieutenant."

"*Would* you now?"

"I have the information you wanted," I told him.

"What information?" he asked, suspiciously.

"About the hit-and-run driver."

"Oh-oh," he said.

"Moreover," I told him, "I can tell you all about the Bishop murder and you can solve both cases. When you come up to see me you'd better have your new uniform on and you'd better come alone."

"How come?"

"The newspapermen will want to take pictures."

"You know, Lam," he said, "there's a lot about you I like, but you have one bad point."

"What's that?"

"You don't know geography. You think this is Los Angeles."

"No, I know where this is."

"You think the kind of stuff that sells real estate in Los Angeles will get you by with the San Francisco police department."

"What do *you* think sells the real estate in Los Angeles?" I asked.

"Meadow mayonnaise," he said.

"You're wrong," I told him. "It's the climate," and hung up.

I didn't have to wait much over ten minutes. He hadn't put on a new uniform but he'd taken a chance that there might be some favorable publicity and had come alone.

I said, "On that hit-and-run business—"

"Oh, yes."

"I have to protect the source of my information."

"I don't like that, Donald."

"But," I said, "if you get a confession, you don't give a damn who gave me the information."

"Not if I get a confession."

I said, "Let's go and get one and then I'll tell you about the Bishop murder case."

"Where are we going?"

I gave him the name and address of Harvey B. Ludlow.

"You know, if this is a bum steer, Donald," he said, "you could be awfully slap-happy when you came into court on a blackmail charge."

I said, "I called you, didn't I?"

"Yes."

"I told you where to come, didn't I?"

"Yes."

"Do I look that dumb?"

"No, you don't look that dumb, but I get fooled every once in a while on you Los Angeles creeps."

I didn't say anything. It was better not to.

We made time in the lieutenant's car.

"How about the Bishop murder?" he asked after a few minutes.

I said, "Let's try the Ludlow business first. If that's pay dirt then you'll be more ready to listen, and if it isn't pay dirt you wouldn't have confidence in anything I said."

"Donald," he said, "if that isn't pay dirt you aren't even going to feel like talking."

We went to the Ludlow residence. Ludlow was in bed.

It was pay dirt.

Harvey B. Ludlow, a fleshy, heavy-set, retired broker, started to shake like cold consommé on a plate when he saw the lieutenant's badge. Before Sheldon had asked half a dozen questions Ludlow was blabbing it all out.

It didn't even need the marks on Ludlow's car by way of confirmation to clinch the case. Ludlow was just aching for an opportunity to spill everything he knew and get it off his chest.

He'd had four or five drinks and had been at a business conference. One of his associates had had his secretary at the conference taking notes, and Ludlow had said he'd take her home.

They stopped for a couple of cocktails, and Ludlow kept looking the secretary over with an appraising eye. She didn't like her job, knew Ludlow had lots of dough, and looked right back at him.

Ludlow didn't tell us *that* angle, but we could see the money angle was the only inducement from a girl's viewpoint he could have had to offer.

By the time Ludlow started for home by way of the girl's apartment, he was feeling the effects of the four or five cocktails, and a sudden surge of self-confidence which made him think he wasn't such a bad-looking old coot after all. The girl was willing to listen to his quavering wolf howls.

That was the story.

Ludlow had wanted to protect his "good name." He saw a chance to get away and he took that chance. He'd been terror-stricken ever since.

He was a prominent clubman and it was going to make enough of a scandal so Lieutenant Sheldon thought he'd better get his captain in on the deal. He got him up out of bed.

The newspaper photographers came out and took pictures of them inspecting Ludlow's car with a microscope, took pictures of Ludlow's wife with her arms around his neck, stating that she'd stand by him through thick and thin, that it had all been a lamentable misunderstanding.

Lieutenant Sheldon and the captain gave the newspaper reporters a great story about how they had carefully worked the thing out by a process of elimination, that they'd made a surreptitious examination of Ludlow's car without his having the least idea that he was an object of police suspicion, that he had been under investigation for some three or four days. That was the way the police worked, quietly, efficiently, but with deadly precision.

It was a beautiful story.

No one even introduced me to the newspaper reporters.

After the pictures had been taken, the captain and Lieutenant Sheldon drove me back to police headquarters.

Sheldon had his arm around my shoulders when we went in. We were buddies. I could have squared all the parking tickets in San Francisco.

We went into the captain's office.

Sheldon said, "I haven't had a chance to explain to you about Donald Lam, Captain."

"He gave you a tip on that Ludlow case?" the captain asked.

Sheldon looked at him reproachfully. "Hell, no," he said. "I did that on my own, but I've been looking for Lam for quite a while."

"Why, Lieutenant?"

"I think he knows something about the Bishop murder."

The captain whistled.

"Mind if I take him in and talk to him for a while in my office, Captain? Would you mind waiting a few minutes longer?"

"Hell, no. Don't you want me along?"

"I think I can do better if Donald and I just sit down and talk things over, sort of palsy-walsy. I don't mind telling you, Captain, I think I know what happened in that case. I think I can go out and put my finger on the murderer right now."

"Well, who is it?"

Lieutenant Sheldon shook his head. "Donald Lam has a couple of facts that I think will clinch the matter, at least I think he has. Give me half an hour with him and then I'll tell you the whole story, and I *hope* I'll have proof."

The captain said, "You come right to me with it, Lieutenant. Don't talk to anyone else. Just talk to Lam and then come right in to me. You understand?"

Lieutenant Sheldon met his eyes. "Of course I understand, Captain."

"You're doing a damn fine job," the captain went on. "That's the kind of an officer I like to have. You think it'll be about half an hour?"

"About half an hour."

"The chief will be interested in this," the captain said.

Sheldon nodded, got up and took my arm. "Come on, Donald," he said. "I think you have some information that'll help. You may not know it'll help but I've got a pretty good theory as to what happened. If I can get a couple of angles from you I think I'll be ready to sew the case up. Be seeing you, Captain."

Chapter Nineteen   •

I said to Lieutenant Sheldon, "We're going to have to get John Carver Billings in here."

"The kid?"

"No, the old man."

He said, "They've got a high-power attorney. He's instructed them not to talk, and—"

"We're going to have to get him in here."

He looked at me and said, "You know, Donald, I've stuck my neck way, way out on this thing, and if I have to go back to the captain in half an hour and tell him 'No soap'— Well, that's going to be tough on me, and it's going to be *awfully* damn tough on you."

I said, "You've got half an hour, Lieutenant. I've shown you what I could do so far. You've got a nice story breaking in the papers tomorrow."

"That's water under the bridge. What have we got for follow-up?"

"That," I said, "depends upon how much confidence you have in me."

He picked up a telephone, dialed one of the interoffice exchanges, and said, "Get John Carver Billings in here— the old man. That's right. Hurry it up. I don't give a damn what his lawyer said; get him in here, now, quick, fast! Wake him up!"

He hung up.

"I'd like to know something about your theory, Donald."

I said, "Listen to what I have to say to Billings. Have a

stenographer ready to take down a confession."

He said, "Donald, if you could crack this—it would be something."

"It's something."

"You mean it's Billings?"

I said, "The homicide squad has already got the dope on Billings."

"A confession from him would be a feather in my cap."

I said, "To hell with a feather, Lieutenant. I'm going to get a whole war bonnet for you, stuck with feathers all up and down the line. Billings didn't have anything to do with the murder."

There was genuine affection in Lieutenant Sheldon's eyes. "Have a cigar, Donald," he said. "These are damned good cigars."

Ten minutes later, John Carver Billings was brought into the office. His lips were clamped in a thin line of firm determination. His eyes looked as though someone had turned out the light, but he was sitting tight.

There was surprise on his face when he saw me sitting there, then he said to Lieutenant Sheldon, "I have been instructed by my attorney to answer no questions except in the presence of my attorney and on the instructions of my attorney."

He sat down.

I said, "Mr. Billings, I think there's a chance to clean this thing up."

He looked at me and recited, "I have been instructed by my attorney to answer no questions except in the presence of my attorney and on the advice of my attorney."

I said, "Don't answer any questions."

"I have been instructed not to talk about anything."

"Don't talk," I said. "Listen."

He shut his mouth and closed his eyes as though trying to withdraw his personality from everything in the office and everything in connection with it.

I said to Lieutenant Sheldon, "Here's what happened, Lieutenant. George Tustin Bishop owned The Green Door. You probably won't want to know anything about it officially, but unofficially you know what that is."

Sheldon said, "I thought a man named Channing was—"

"Channing," I said, "was Bishop's accountant when he started in. He moved in and cut himself a piece of cake when he found out what was going on.

"Bishop posed as a mining man. He didn't want to fail to report his income but he didn't want to report it as coming from a gambling place. Therefore he worked a lot of dummy corporations and he developed mines, shipped ore to smelting companies, got checks from smelting companies, and all of that. If anybody had ever taken the trouble to investigate, the whole thing would have been turned up, but no one took the trouble to investigate because the books were all regular on their face. It just never occurred to anyone that a smelting company would be willing to pay gold-ore prices for common dirt. And there was always one mine named 'The Green Door.' "

"Go ahead," Sheldon said.

I said, "Before Bishop got into the gambling business he'd been doing a little blackmailing on the side. I don't know whether he'd blackmailed anyone other than Billings's son, but he'd been coming down pretty hard on the boy. I don't know just what he had on him. I haven't gone that far, but I think before we get done Mr. Billings, here, will tell us what it was."

Sheldon glanced inquiringly at Billings.

Billings was sitting there with his eyes tightly shut and his fists clenched, his mouth pushed together as though he were afraid some word might inadvertently spill out when he didn't want it to. His face was the color of wet concrete.

I said, "After Bishop got into The Green Door he didn't

care so much about blackmail. That was penny-ante stuff. But, remember, Bishop had something on young Billings. He knew it and Channing probably knew it. Channing may not have known what it was.

"Anyway, Channing started moving in on the business and Bishop didn't like that. Bishop became a little worried about Channing. He needed some dummy whom he could trust to carry on the business end of things, but Channing was rapidly getting himself in the position where Bishop couldn't trust him and Bishop was about ready to see that Channing got put away where he couldn't and wouldn't talk.

"Then Gabby Garvanza decided he'd move in. Someone filled him full of lead and didn't do a good job of it."

"Know who it was?" Sheldon asked.

"Sure. It was George Bishop. He thought he'd done a good job of it at the time. When he read in the morning papers that Gabby would recover, he almost passed out. His widow will confirm that."

The lieutenant nodded. "Go on, Lam."

I said, "Bishop had been sweet on Maurine Auburn at one time. Channing had introduced Maurine to Gabby Garvanza, then Bishop married Irene, the strip-tease artist, and Maurine teamed up with Gabby; but Maurine kept carrying the torch for Bishop.

"Then Bishop and Gabby Garvanza got at cross-purposes. Bishop tried to put him out of the way and it was an amateurish job. Bishop was a gambler and a blackmailer but not a killer. He didn't do a neat, workmanlike job.

"When Bishop partially recovered from the shock of finding that Gabby was still with us, he decided he had to make another pass at Gabby before Gabby got ready to move around."

"Go ahead," Sheldon said.

I said, "Bishop wanted Maurine to put Gabby on the spot where they'd be sure Gabby didn't escape the next time, so it was all fixed up that Maurine was to get a little bit crocked and impulsive and fall for a handsome stranger. The stranger was in reality an aviator who was hired by Bishop but was really Channing's man. It had to be that way. You can't account for what happened on any other theory. Channing knew Bishop was getting restless; he decided he'd better beat Bishop to the punch. He also knew that gambling houses don't go through probate."

"Okay, tell me about the aviator," he said.

"The aviator took instructions from Bishop, but reported to Channing. That aviator picked Maurine up and flew her right fast up to a field north of San Francisco where Bishop was waiting.

"The only trouble was Channing was waiting, too.

"Maurine climbed into the car with Bishop. Channing slipped up behind. There were two guns. The one that killed Maurine was an automatic. We haven't traced that yet. The gun that killed Bishop was one that Channing had thoughtfully slipped out of the cabin of the Billings yacht. And a bullet hole with bloody tissue around it was thoughtfully left by the murderer as a clue."

Sheldon broke in. "You mean Channing shot Bishop a second time on Billings's yacht?"

"Yes, so it would lodge in the paneling of the cabin. A bullet hole with bloody tissue around it would be pretty damning evidence.

"In the meantime, Bishop had been trying to put a squeeze on Billings, not a money blackmail, but Bishop wanted a favor. It was a favor that Billings didn't want to grant."

"What favor?" Sheldon asked.

I said, "The pitcher that goes to the well too often gets broken. The salesman who keeps on ringing doorbells sooner or later is bound to get an order."

"I don't get you," Sheldon said.

I said, "Bishop had been playing around with gold mines, shipping the dirt out and using it for ballast or dumping it in the bay. The last bunch of dirt he dumped on his lot in order to build up a terraced garden. It was pay dirt. It runs about three hundred dollars to the ton of free-milling ore. It isn't rich enough so you can see the gold sticking out all over it, but the gold's there. You break it up and pan out the gold and you really get a surprise."

Lieutenant Sheldon thought that over.

I gave him a minute, then went on. "Bishop controlled the majority stock. Some of it had been sold to the public. Most of it was being held in escrow.

"You see, the way Bishop operated, he needed a successive string of corporations. He'd get permission to sell stock by having it held in escrow for a year. Then the corporation would go to mining.

"Before the year was out, a board of experts would appraise the mine as valueless and Bishop would send out this report, apparently unwillingly but under a directive of the corporation commission.

"Naturally the suckers would draw back their escrow stock money and the promoter would be left with his stock—and *then,* after everyone had forgotten about the mine, the income from the 'smelting company' would start rolling in. The books would show credit to The Green Door. There'd always be a mine by that name. No income tax man ever went any deeper than that. It was a natural. And if there'd ever been a stink, Bishop could have shown he'd reported every cent of income from The Green Door as coming from The Green Door. No one could ask for more than that. If the income tax people thought it was from the mine, Bishop couldn't be blamed for their mistake."

"Okay, so then he struck pay dirt?"

"Exactly. And it was in a mining company where the name happened to appeal to the public. That made the background of this particular company entirely different.

"No mining experts could possibly report this mine as being 'unprofitable.'

"Bishop wanted to get all that stock back and he wanted it back at prices that came nowhere near reflecting the true value, so he asked Billings to have the bank file suit against the corporation on the note that Bishop had signed with the corporation. Billings smelled a rat. He wouldn't do it. But Bishop had this hold on Billings. He used that lever to get what he wanted.

"Channing knew the inside. When he decided to put Bishop out of the way, he wanted to be sure that the murder was pinned on Billings. If the police didn't have any good clues, then Channing would be the most likely suspect.

"Horace B. Catlin is a man I don't know much about. He's a member of the yacht club. I presume he's in financial difficulties. Anyway, he got hanging around The Green Door and probably got in pretty deep. Channing didn't report that to Bishop. He held out so he could use Catlin for his own purpose.

"Tuesday evening Catlin discharged his obligation to Channing. He loaned Channing his yacht. Channing transferred Bishop's body to Catlin's yacht and moved Bishop's automobile to a side road. An airplane took Maurine's body down south, so it would appear to police that the torpedo who had tried to rub out Gabby Garvanza had shot Maurine so she couldn't tell the police what she knew.

"The idea was to have her buried where the body would be found—after a while.

"But Bishop's body was to be dumped right into Billings's lap. That way police would never suspect Channing.

"The yacht club keeps a close watch on people who come in through the gate and people who go out through the gate, but it doesn't pay any attenion to the people who come in by yacht and the people who go out by yacht. They're all members in good standing who have already cleared through the gate. That's all there was to it. Channing brought Catlin's yacht into the club, then, after it got dark, he picked the lock on Billings's boat, put Bishop's body aboard, and pulled what turned out to be the slickest stunt of all—he dropped the gun, with which Bishop had been killed, overboard, knowing that Billings would never think to look for the gun in case he found the body. But Channing knew that the police would send a diver down to look for the weapon the first thing they did."

"It's a nice story," Lieutenant Sheldon said.

I said, "Channing must have planned to have the body 'discovered' a day or two later, but Billings beat him to it. Billings and his dad went down to the yacht club for something. They just happened to get aboard with no one seeing them because the electric signal had been jammed, and Danby, the watchman, had his back turned to them and was talking on the telephone when they came in.

"When they found Bishop's body they knew that they were up against it. They knew that once Bishop's body was found there the scandal that he had used as a blackmail lever would come out, and they also knew they'd be accused of murder. So they tried to get rid of the evidence. They did a clumsy, bungling, amateurish job. They first had to get rid of the body. They managed to move it over to one of the adjoining yachts. In order to do that they had to smash the lock. They were afraid the watchman would notice the smashed lock, so they bought another lock. There was blood on the carpet. They took up the old carpet and put down new carpet. Everything they did put their heads that much farther into the noose."

Lieutenant Sheldon's face was suddenly grim.

"Okay, Donald, *who* hired *you*?"

"John Carver Billings."

"The old man?"

"The kid."

He said, "You son of a bitch," with such concentrated venom in his voice that it made Bertha Cool's epithets sound like love pats.

"What's the matter?" I asked.

"Trying to sell me a bill of goods like this," he said. "You sleuthed out the Ludlow hit-and-run case so you could build up a credit, and then, after you had me sold, you came along with this cock-and-bull story."

I said, "Wait a minute, Lieutenant."

"Wait, hell! You've shot your wad, Donald. You tried to pull a fast one and I'm going to show you just what happens to slick bastards like you that try to—"

"Now shut up," I said, "and forget you're a damn cop. You have the captain waiting in there, and by this time the captain has probably given the chief a buzz and told him to stand by because he thinks he's got a solution of the Bishop murder coming up. Now do you want to use your head or lose it?"

He winced at my reference to the captain and the chief. He was in one hell of a spot and he knew it.

"Donald," he said, with such an intensity of hatred his voice was actually so low as to be all but inaudible, "for a double cross like this I could break every bone in your body."

I said, "You've got one way of checking this story. You've got about twenty minutes left in which to do it. That's to get Horace B. Catlin in here and—"

Lieutenant Sheldon spun the dial on the phone. A couple of uniformed men were in the office before one would have thought it was possible to get a connection. He said, "Keep these guys where nobody can see them. I don't give a damn who it is. Don't let *anybody* see them. Don't let them talk with anyone in the department. Don't let them talk with any lawyers. Don't let them talk with anyone outside the department. Don't let them get to a telephone. Sew them up. Keep them right here."

Lieutenant Sheldon went out of the office like a jet plane taking off on a trial run.

Billings opened his eyes and looked at me. Slowly he reached out and shook hands with me.

He didn't say a word.

I said, "*Don't* tell them what it was Bishop had on your son, and—"

"Shut up," one of the officers said. "The lieutenant said you weren't to talk to anyone."

"Well, that didn't mean we couldn't talk with each other."

"That ain't the way I understood it. Shut up."

Billings started to say something. One of the cops moved over.

"You boys can get yourselves pretty badly hurt," he said, "by sticking your necks out."

We sat there in silence.

It was a long thirty minutes. I guessed I looked at my watch fifty times, but Billings just sat there motionless, wooden-faced.

Then Lieutenant Sheldon came in. His face looked like the face of a ten-year-old kid on Christmas morning. I looked at it and let out a long-drawn sigh of relief.

"Donald," he said, "run over that line again so I can get the straight of it. The captain's waiting and the chief is in his office. You two mugs get the hell out of here."

The uniformed men withdrew.

I ran over it once more for Lieutenant Sheldon's benefit.

"How did you spot Catlin?"

"I knew there must be some member of the yachting-club who was completely in the power of the man who was managing The Green Door. Such a man must be a plunger who had got in so deep he had to follow instructions.

"I simply got the caretaker at the yacht club to keep a watch on The Green Door. When a member of the club went in, I figured he was my man.

"I followed him in. When I realized he wasn't playing at any of the tables but was undoubtedly closeted with the manager, I felt certain I had the answer I wanted."

"Have a cigar," Lieutenant Sheldon said to me. "Have another one. Here, Billings, have a cigar. We're awfully sorry we had to inconvenience you, sir, but you understand how it is. You fellows wait here. Don't try to go out. There'll be a guard in the corridor. Just sit here and don't talk to anybody. Donald, you're smart enough to keep your mouth shut. See that Billings keeps his shut. *Don't see any reporters. Don't try to use the phone.* We may be able to do something for you guys."

Lieutenant Sheldon spun the dial on the telephone and when he had an answer said, "I'm coming right up, Captain. Sorry to keep you waiting. There was one other angle I had to check on. I'll be right in."

He dashed out of the office.

I turned to Billings. "What was it Bishop had on your son?" I asked.

He said, "Honestly, Lam, I didn't know until a week ago. I prefer not to discuss it."

"You'd better tell me."

"I'll be damned if I do."

I said, "Your son is a tall, rangy lad."

He nodded.

"Play any basketball in college?"

"Yes."

"He was on the college team?"

"Yes."

I said, "Bishop was a gambler who made book on college games."

The banker's face suddenly twisted. He began to cry. It was something to watch, the spectacle of a hard man whose tear ducts had all dried up twisting his face into a contortion of grief.

I got up and went to a window, turning my back. A few minutes later, when the sobbing had stopped, I went back and sat down.

For a long while neither one of us said anything.

After a while I said, "When you tell your story to Sheldon tell him your boy was mixed up in a scandal over a girl."

"That wouldn't be a powerful enough motive," Billings said. "I've been thinking of that."

"Tell him the girl died as the result of a criminal operation."

Billings thought that over for a moment, then nodded thoughtfully. "Donald," he said, "if you can get the police to adopt your story as the official version of what happened, you're going to be very handsomely rewarded, *very* handsomely rewarded."

I'd been associating with Bertha long enough so I looked him straight in the eyes and said, "We would expect that, Mr. Billings. We don't work for nothing, you know."

"You don't have to," he said.

That covered all the conversation. There wasn't anything more to be said.

We sat there and waited and waited.

After a couple of hours an officer came in with sandwiches and a pot of coffee. He said, "The lieutenant wanted me to tell you to make yourselves comfortable. He said not to do any talking."

We had the coffee and sandwiches. About an hour later Lieutenant Sheldon came in, closed the door, pulled up his chair, and sat clown close to Billings.

"Mr. Billings," he said, "you're an important man in San Francisco, and we want you to know that the police recognize your importance. We try to give the important citizens a break whenever we can."

"Thank you," Billings said.

"Now, then, Bishop had something on your son. Would you mind telling us what it was?"

"It was over a girl," Billings said.

Lieutenant Sheldon merely grinned.

"The girl had an operation and died."

The grin came off Sheldon's face. He thought that over for some little time.

"All right, Mr. Billings," he said, "I think we can keep the blackmail angle out of it if you'll co-operate with us."

"If you'll keep that angle out of it," Billings said, "I'll— I'll do anything, anything in the world."

"All right," Sheldon said. "There's only one thing you need to do."

"What's that?"

"Protect us in our efforts to protect you."

"What do you mean?"

"Don't do any talking. These newspaper men are pretty damned smart. They'll cross-examine you if you ever give them the ghost of a chance. They'll question you and then check up on the answers. They'll get you cornered and—"

"You don't want me to give them anything, is that it?" Billings interrupted.

"For your own good," the lieutenant hastened to interpose. "Mind you, we're trying to give you a break. There's only one possible way we can keep this blackmail angle out of it."

"I'll keep quiet," Billings said.

"You see," Sheldon said, beaming, "if you co-operate

with the police, they'll co-operate with you."

I turned to Sheldon and said, "One thing you could do for me, Lieutenant."

"Anything, Donald, anything you want. The whole damn city is yours. Just anything you want."

I said, "In giving the story to the newspapers you could emphasize the fact that George Bishop had struck it rich in that mine."

He looked at me and grinned. "Bless your soul, Donald," he said. "The story is in print already. The rich gold mine is a smash hit. It's dramatic. I've talked to so damn many reporters I'm hoarse. Now, Donald, *you'll* want to remain in the background in this thing. You'll want to have it so that any time you have another case in San Francisco you can count on the co-operation of the whole damn police department. That's the way you want it, isn't it?"

I nodded.

He came over and clapped his hand on my shoulder so that it all but knocked the breath out of me.

"Donald," he said, "you're a smart boy. You're going places. Believe me, you haven't done yourself a damn bit of harm on *this* case. Anything you want in San Francisco you can get, and that's something that not many private agencies can say—particularly if they have headquarters in Los Angeles."

He laughed at that one.

"How about me?" Billings asked. "And what about my boy? Are we free to—"

"Oh, I forgot to tell you," Sheldon said. "We've been so damned busy. We got your chauffeur up out of bed, Mr. Billings, and your limousine is waiting right out at the front door. Now, tere'll be a lot of newspaper reporters taking flashlights when you get in the car. They'll ask you a lot of questions. If you just say, 'No comment,' it will help a lot. We don't want to get at cross-purposes. If you want to keep that blackmail angle out of the papers it would be a lot better to let me do *all* the talking."

"There isn't anything I want to talk about," Billings said.

"Well, that's all there is to it," Sheldon said, and grabbed Billings's hand in an ecstasy of cordiality.

He escorted Billings to the door, held it open, and then let his thick arm bar my exit.

He said, "You'd better let Mr. Billings go out alone, Donald. His son will join him down there at the car and there'll be a lot of photographers. It might be better if *you* didn't have *your* picture taken in the group. You know how it is. You fellows can work a lot better if people don't know anything at all about you."

"That's me," I told him, "a passion for anonymity."

Sheldon said to Billings, "And you'd better see this fellow gets a damn good fee, Mr. Billings. Believe me, he's been a lot of help to us in this case and a lot of help to you."

"Don't worry," Billings said. "I wasn't born yesterday."

The door closed.

"Isn't there a back way out of here?" I asked Sheldon.

He clapped me on the back so hard that I had a job catching my breath.

"Donald, it's a pleasure to co-operate with a private detective who *really* knows his way around. *Anything* we can do for you at *any* time we're only too glad to do, *anything* at all. Come on out, right this way."

Daylight was just breaking as he eased me out through the ambulance entrance in the back. A police car took me to my hotel.

Chapter Twenty

I walked into the office.

The receptionist looked up, gave a start as though she'd seen a ghost, and put a finger over her lips, motioning for silence. She jerked her thumb toward Bertha Cool's office.

I moved over to the desk. "What's the matter? Bertha on the warpath?"

"Bertha wanted to be notified as soon as you came in."

"Was that the way she expressed it?"

"Not exactly."

"How did she express it?"

"Bertha said, 'If that slimy little worm has nerve enough to stick his nose in the door, you call me and I'll throw him out myself. The partnership's dissolved.' "

"Nice of her," I said. "Give her a ring. Tell her I just came in, and am in my private office."

I moved over to my office door.

The gilt letters reading *Donald Lam* on the frosted glass had been crudely and violently scratched off. I figured Bertha had gone to work with the nearest safety-razor blade, nicking it in the process.

Elsie Brand looked up at me with wide-eyed incredulity. "Donald," she said, "don't, don't come here! Go see a lawyer and have him— My God, Donald, there's going to be a scene."

I took a cashier's check from my pocket and said, "I wanted to repay the money you sent me, Elsie."

"That's all right, Donald, that's all right. Don't let Bertha know I sent it. Donald, what's this? This is for thirteen—thirteen— Donald, this is for *thirteen thousand dollars!*"

"That's right."

"A cashier's check," she said.

"That's right. Billings's bank."

"But what— But what—"

"I invested the money you sent in mining stock," I said. "The Skyhook Mining and Development Syndicate, a nice company. It looked like a good buy, and after we had the stock bought, it went up like a skyrocket. I sold out to a syndicate that's taking over the whole mine."

"Donald, you mean my three hundred and fifty— Donald, I don't understand."

"You don't have to," I said, "Just cash the check and—"

It felt as though an earthquake were rocking the office building on its foundations. Somewhere in the outer office a chair tipped over, a desk was shoved to one side and slammed against the partition as though it had been hurled by some giant hand, the door almost ripped off its hinges, and Bertha Cool stood there on the threshold, her eyes glittering, her voice raised so that it was audible all over the office, and well out into the corridor.

"You double-crossing, pint-sized barnacle of frustration! You've got a crust to come in here. Why, you've got no more right here than a moth in a clothes closet. You little two-bit, skinny-necked, flat-chested, dimple-waisted, beetle-browed, double-crossing bastard—

"What a master mind *you* turned out to be!

"After Bertha had five hundred dollars safely tucked away *you* went up to San Francisco and stuck your peanut brain into the thing! *You* pushed *your* nose into the business and what happened? They stopped payment on that check! You and your big mouth! You and your master mind!

"Then you get our clients arrested for murder. Now we're listed as blackmailers in San Francisco. And the police want you. There's a pickup order out for you. Think of that! A pickup for a Los Angeles private detective, a partner of mine. I picked you out of the gutter. I took you in here and gave you a partnership. Why, you— Fry me for an oyster!"

She turned around and yelled over her shoulder to the girl at the telephone desk, "Get police headquarters on the line and tell them Donald Lam is waiting for his steel bracelets. Tell them the master mind of the whole damn detective profession is back here, waiting."

She put her hands on her hips, her elbows thrust far out, her jaw pushed forward like a bulldog.

I said, "You'll have to sign here, Bertha," and scaled a card across the desk at her.

She didn't even look down at the card. "Sign my fanny!" she said. "Before I sign anything for you it'll take an order from the Supreme Court.

"And don't think you've got a damn cent coming. You've raised enough hell with the business so that it'll take every cent of assets to compensate for the damage. I've talked with my lawyer and he says I'm dead right. Go get yourself a lawyer and see how much good it does you.

"The personal things that were cleaned out of your desk are in that cardboard box in the corner. Now, get the hell out of here."

I said, "You'd better sign that card, Bertha. It's the new partnership bank account in San Francisco."

"A partnership account? What the hell have you been doing? Signing checks? Damn you, Donald, you'll go to prison. I stopped payment on any check bearing your signature. I cleaned out the partnership bank account and redeposited it in my individual name. I've dissolved the partnership. I picked you up out of the gutter and, so help me, I'm going to drop you back *into* the gutter."

I said, "That's all right. Then I'll take over the San Francisco bank account. You keep the business here in Los Angeles if you want. You won't need to bother about legal stuff. If the partnership was dissolved, the money I made up there then becomes my individual—"

"The money you *made* up there?"

"That's right."

She grabbed the card and looked at it, said, "Why, this is just a banking card in the San Francisco bank for signatures on the partnership account of Cool and Lam."

"That's right," I said. "There was quite a bit of money up there so I decided we'd better have a San Francisco bank account. After all, we're in good with the San Francisco police and they're going to send us all the business they can. Anything we get with a San Francisco angle will be handled up there as though we were the mayor's partners."

"What the hell are you talking about?" she said.

"You knew the Bishop murder case was solved?"

"*Was* solved is right," she said. "Don't try to tell me you had anything to do with that. I read the newspapers. Of all the damned, botched-up messes. You stuck your neck out and got Billings mixed up in it and damn near ruined his reputation. My God, if Billings sues us for damages and—"

"He won't," I said. "He gave me a check for five thousand dollars."

"For five thousand dollars?"

"That's right. Previous to that time he'd given me a check for fifteen hundred dollars for expenses."

"He gave *you* a check for fifteen hundred dollars for expenses?"

"That's right."

"Stew me for a clam!" Bertha said in an awed voice.

"From the way you describe it," I said, "I gather that check was after the partnership had been dissolved."

Bertha blinked her eyes at me. Suddenly she said, "How much is in the San Francisco bank?"

I said, "The five thousand dollars that I collected from Billings by way of a fee is there. In addition to that, the expense money he gave me I invested in mining stock."

Bertha's face became even more purple. "You took expense money and put it in—in—in mining stock? Why, you canary-brained, pint-sized bastard. I could take you— Why, damn you, that's embezzlement. I could— Get the police! Get the police. I'm going to make a complaint myself," she screamed over her shoulder.

"And then," I went on, "I sold the stock at a neat little profit. We cleaned up something like forty thousand. My broker was able to corner just about all the outstanding stock in the Skyhook Mining and Development Syndicate. We haven't got the bill for long-distance telephones yet. It'll probably be several hundred dollars, but we got the stock and we made a cleanup. We—"

Bertha's jaw was sagging as though I'd hit her in the face with a wet towel. "You— You what?"

"Of course, when I say I sold out at a profit, Bertha, you understand that's before taxes. We'll have to pay income tax on this. I didn't think it was safe to hold it long enough to go for a capital gains. It was one of those stock deals where you want to get in fast and out fast. However, I did hang on to a small block of stock so that if it should go up much higher we could hang on and take a capital gains."

Bertha grabbed up the white card with the banking imprint and the blank for signatures. She jerked a fountain pen out of Elsie Brand's desk set, then suddenly remembered and stepped back into the outer office.

"What the hell are *you* doing?" she screamed at the girl at the reception desk. "Hang up that damned phone."

Bertha plumped herself down in a chair and scrawled her signature just over mine on the banking card.

"Elsie, darling," she said, "you send that right up to San Francisco, right away. Send it up to the bank."

She looked up at me and took a deep breath. Her rage-purpled lips twisted into a grin.

"Donald, lover," she said, "you *do* upset Bertha's nerves terribly at times. You know Bertha's irritable, and there are times when she doesn't understand just what you're doing. You ought to keep in closer touch with Bertha.

"Come into the office and tell me all about it, Donald, lover, and Elsie, you get that jerk of a sign painter and tell him to get Donald Lam's name back on the door before noon. And get the things out of that cardboard box and have them all put back in Donald's desk just like they were. I'll hold you personally responsible if Donald is inconvenienced the least little bit.

"Now, Donald, you need a rest. You've been going day and night. How you stand it Bertha will never know.

"You come right into Bertha's office, lover, and tell her all that happened. Come right on in, lover."

Elsie Brand pushed a postcard across the desk toward me. "I thought you might like your mail before you went in, Mr. Lam," she said.

I picked up the postcard. It was an airmail postcard from Havana, Cuba. It was addressed to me personally and it said:

Darling: Having a wonderful time. Wish you were here.
                                Millie.

The words, *Wish you were here,* had been heavily underscored.

Bertha Cool slipped an affectionate arm around me. "Come on in, you little bastard," she said. "Tell Big Bertha all about that forty thousand bucks. You brainy little son of a bitch."

THE
END